T0275419

# The Boy in the Earth

**Books by Fuminori Nakamura**

*The Thief*
*Evil and the Mask*
*Last Winter, We Parted*
*The Gun*
*The Kingdom*
*The Boy in the Earth*
*Cult X*
*My Annihilation*
*The Rope Artist*

# The
# Boy
# in the
# Earth

**FUMINORI NAKAMURA**

Translated from the Japanese by

**ALLISON MARKIN POWELL**

Copyright © 2005 by Fuminori Nakamura
English translation copyright © 2017 by Allison Markin Powell
English translation rights arranged with Shinchosa Publishing
Co., Ltd., through the English Agency Japan, Ltd.
First published in Japanese by Shinchosha Publishing Co., Ltd,
under the title 土の中の子ども, *Tsuchi no naka no kodomo*.

First published in English by Soho Press, Inc.
Soho Press
227 W 17th Street
New York, NY 10011

All rights reserved.

Library of Congress Cataloging-in-Publication Data

Nakamura, Fuminori, 1977– author.
Powell, Allison Markin, translator.
The boy in the earth / Fuminori Nakamura
translated by Allison Markin Powell.
Other titles: *Tsuchi no naka no kodomo*

ISBN 978-1-61695-895-4
eISBN 978-1-61695-595-3

1. Fathers and sons—Japan—Tokyo—Fiction.
2. Adult child abuse victims—Japan—Tokyo—Fiction.
I. Title
PL873.5.A339 T7813 2017  895.63'6—dc23  2016044296

Interior design by Janine Agro

Printed in the United States of America

10 9 8 7 6 5 4 3 2

# The Boy in the Earth

1

In the flood of headlights surrounding me, I saw that there was no escape. The motorcycles were just gunning their engines and watching me as I stood there, helpless to do anything. But I doubted that this standoff would go on for much longer. I figured soon these guys would get off their bikes and beat me with the iron pipes they were holding until they were satisfied.

Fear had made my legs go unpleasantly weak,

but for some time now, I had been distracted by the thought that I must have been expecting all of this to happen. Until just a little while ago, I had been aimlessly wandering around the late night streets with no destination, smoking as I walked. It was as if I had been searching for the city's darkest places, bidden by the poorly lit streets. I had encountered these guys in front of a vending machine beside a park. They had stopped their bikes and were still sitting astride them, drinking juice, munching away and smoking cigarettes like they were drunk. At first, they hadn't paid attention to me. They had been cheerfully howling with laughter—that is, until I threw my cigarette butt toward them.

I did what I did on purpose—with clear intention. It was not unconscious, nor was it for no reason at all—I was completely cognizant and aware of my actions. It was something I had to do, show these dregs of society what I thought of them, hanging out in a place like this. Those were my thoughts at the time. But now, awash in the light of their motorcycles, I could not fathom why I had felt that way.

There was no question, though, that here I found

myself in a predicament. I had done something stupid without thinking of the consequences—that was all there was to it—but this kind of thing happened to me with some regularity. Just the day before yesterday, a car was making a right-hand turn against the light, and, for no reason other than to demonstrate how dangerous it was, instead of trying to avoid it I deliberately stopped in the middle the crosswalk, right in front of the car so that the driver had no choice but to slam on the brakes. What both these instances had in common was that the direct result of my own actions put me in danger—it was my own behavior that thrust me into unfavorable conditions.

"Hey, what do you think you're doing?" A guy with a shaved head who was most likely the leader got off his bike, his eyes unfocused. The others were still revving their engines, like in a kind of ritual. When the leader raised the iron pipe, his expression was hollow, as if he had no interest in what might happen to my body when he brought the pipe down. The blow landed on my side with an unexpectedly intense pain that knocked the wind out of me, and a moment later an unbearable jolt of searing heat coursed through my entire body. I found it difficult to breathe—I barely managed to inhale through my constricted throat. A frail, inside-out voice leaked from my lips. The shivers of pain and fear that wracked my body would not stop. I tried to stand up, but my ankle and knee joints were so stiff they didn't seem to work.

"Your money, all of it. And then, right . . . t-ten more of those and we'll let you go!" he said and, as if waiting to see what I would do, he lit a cigarette. All I had on me at the time were a few coins that probably didn't even add up to a thousand yen. Still, I shook my head. I tried to speak, but my face felt like it was on fire, and the next thing I knew, I was lying facedown on the ground. It felt cool against my cheeks, and the blood flowing from my gums leaked out of my mouth in a trickle. I thought they might have lost interest by now, but the situation remained unchanged. I passed out, but just briefly—there was only a momentary gap in my consciousness.

"I guess it's too much trouble to kill him."

"We can't let him get away with this."

"Well, there's no one here to see, and nobody knows us here either."

At some point the sound of the engines had stopped. I could tell that several of the bikers were looking down at me. As I caught the scent of earth, I was seized by a strange sensation. My chest was buzzing with an unfamiliar feeling—it was deep within, though I was definitely aware of it—a feeling stirred by an anxiety that I never could have anticipated. This fear seemed to overwhelm my entire body. A faint smile cracked across my lips. If they kept kicking me, if they beat me to a pulp, I might vanish into nothing, I might be absorbed by the earth, deep underground. It was terrifying. I felt robbed of my strength, and my heart raced painfully, although the twitching that ran up and down my spine was not unpleasant. Little by little, this fearful trembling was transforming into something else entirely, like a feeling of anticipation. Despite my terror, there was the definite sensation that I was patiently standing by. I experienced a moment of skepticism, but then it no longer mattered. I worried about when these guys, all of them together, would start swinging their iron pipes at me again. I had the illusion of my body falling down, down, from a very high place. I worried about the impact when I hit bottom . . .

"Hey, wait a sec. What if while we had this guy, what if we called up a girl he knows on his cell phone and got her to come out here?"

"Sounds good, since we missed our chance before, right?"

"Right."

"Cool. Yeah, let's do it."

I felt a crushing sense of disappointment. "What's wrong with me?" I cried out nonsensically. They were quiet for a moment but soon they all erupted in laughter. I felt a pain in my side, and as my head was pushed down, my mouth filled with earth. They felt around in the pockets of my pants. A quiet disappointment spread through me. All they took was the coin wallet I was carrying, my cigarettes, and a lighter.

"Loser. Hey, this guy's a loser."

"We should kill him."

"Wait, no, there's no point in killing him."

"Shut up, what do you care?"

"Hey, hang on a minute. If you kill him, then we're really fucked."

As they kicked me all over, I drifted out of awareness. Illuminated by the headlights of their motorcycles, I was a mere worm as I let them beat me mercilessly. I was in a state of excitement. I knew that was not an appropriate way to feel in this situation. I don't mean that I experienced a masochistic pleasure from the pain of being kicked. Their attack was relentless; I felt only intense pain. Neither was there any intoxication from feeling worthless. How can I put it?—I was definitely waiting for something yet to come. I felt certain that the thing I was waiting for—whatever it was—was there. It was still unclear to me. But what loomed in my mind was that I may have been expecting it all along.

"There's something strange about the noises this guy's making,"

"He's so funny, look at him."

Their voices sounded far away, yet they didn't let up. I felt an especially hard blow, and my mind began to sway to a strange rhythm. I felt as though my being was about to fracture—my vision blurred, and as an unbearable nausea came over me, I sputtered out vomit. But I did not want to lose consciousness yet. If

I blacked out, that would be the end. Whatever it was would never arrive. This was my thought as I opened my eyes to feel the pain. If I could go on like this, maybe I could transform myself. But into what, I had no idea. I let out a scream. Even though it was my own voice, the cry that echoed in my head sounded unfamiliar.

2

Sayuko opened the door and looked dubiously at me when I came out to greet her. I couldn't tell from her expression whether she was worried about the brutal attack that I had suffered, or if it was just unpleasant to see a guy with a face all swollen up like mine. I thought about asking where she had been but it didn't seem worth the trouble. Her body gave off a strong odor of alcohol.

"Did you get in a fight or something?"

"Yeah. It happened before I knew what was going on."

"With just one guy?"

"No, I think there were about ten of them . . ." I said, and she frowned, her gaze still focused on me.

Last night I had eventually blacked out, then managed to drag myself back to my apartment. My body was in less pain than I'd have thought it would be. Once I'd lost consciousness, the bikers probably thought I was dead and took off. On the way home, I realized that I didn't want to get myself into this kind of situation anymore. I had lost all interest in whatever it was I had been expecting to find. All that was left was melancholy and an indistinct exhaustion. I didn't feel any particular sexual desire at that moment, but I didn't want to be questioned, either, so I brought Sayuko to the bed right after she got home. She lay there with her eyes open, watching my every move without any emotion. Impervious to sex, she did not make a sound during the act itself.

SIX MONTHS AGO, when I had quit my job in sales at a company that produced educational materials,

Sayuko had also lost her part-time job there as a clerk because of a personnel reduction. It had been diffi-cult for her to work there and still keep her night job, so I think she would have quit anyway, but she had resented the company for letting her go first. I had run into her again at a bar where she was having a shouting match with some guy. She had no money and no place to stay. She had lost her apartment when she broke up with the guy at the bar.

So I took Sayuko home with me and we had sex, but the whole time, she just stared vacantly at the ceiling. If was as if she had resigned herself to sleeping with a guy if she were going to live with him. I made every effort to diminish her frigidity, but the result was always the same. She had gotten pregnant and dropped out of university, the guy had found another girlfriend and run off somewhere. Nevertheless, she had resolved to have the baby, but when the child was stillborn, she stopped feeling anything, she told me.

"A long time ago, someone said that the stillborn baby must be the reason why. That I started to hate sex itself from the shock of what happened—that must be why I was rejecting it. What do you think? Are people that uncomplicated? Does that really happen?" she had once asked me.

"Yeah, I guess so," I'd responded noncommittally.

She had muttered, as if to herself, "Then people are just so boring."

AFTER I FINISHED having sex, she lit a cigarette. She stared up at the ceiling as she exhaled the smoke, and it seemed as though she were going to say something to me, but she was silent. My flushed cheeks hurt and, thinking I would cool them off, I wet a towel in the kitchen. Still, I had the feeling I was doing this to try to gloss over the silence, which only made me feel worse. The echo of the water from the faucet was unnecessarily loud in the hushed apartment.

Deliberately, as if to break the silence, she said, "I was drinking with a friend until late." She went on, "I know I just called him a friend, but I meant someone I used to work with at the cabaret club. He offered to treat me . . . You know, the club we went to together."

"I see." I had meant to respond more firmly, but I couldn't help it—I felt drowsy and lethargic.

"Hey, have you really been going to work? Lately you always get home at a slightly different time, you know."

As usual, she had changed the subject quickly.

"They gave me time off for some reason. But I'm going back next week."

"Driving a taxi doesn't pay much, does it? Are you sure it's okay to take time off? If you don't have any money, I'll have to find someone else to pick me up, won't I?" she said, laughing softly and placing the towel on my cheek. She got dimples when she laughed. It was as if they were the only part of her that remained unaffected by her life—her dimples seemed childlike and incongruous on her. After sex, she became more and more talkative, as if she could pursue her own goals starting now.

"I used to know a guy who was a regular salaryman—he suddenly quit his job, and he just stayed in his apartment, doing nothing."

"Really?"

"Then he turned into a molester."

"A molester?"

"Yeah. On the Saikyo Line in the mornings and evenings, almost every day. But he got arrested, and even though he managed to settle out of court, afterward he started getting high on drugs."

"Then what?"

"He ran out of money, he started working as a male escort, but he still didn't have enough cash, so he sold one of his kidneys."

"I wonder how much he got for it."

"I don't know. Then his body gave out and he went to the hospital, where they found out he was a drug addict, so he went to jail. I don't know where he is now."

"I'd like to know what came after."

"Why?"

"What happened to the guy after that? I don't know—I guess it's like, I wonder where a person's lowest point is. I mean, how far are they willing to go?" I said, and she laughed.

"There are plenty of strange people, and they don't need anything to make them act that way—people who seem like they're just trying to be bad. The last time I saw him, this guy was smiling like an idiot, pleased as punch. Was there something that made him be like that, was it his childhood or something? Or maybe it was just that he wanted to be that way, plain and simple."

"He wanted to be that way?"

"Yeah. As in, he wanted to become bad—you know what I mean? Look, don't lemmings commit mass suicide? It's like there are humans who are programmed with that kind of instinct, too."

Somehow this conversation gave me the impression that she had specifically prepared these things to say to me.

"Hmm . . . I don't know."

"But don't you think that would be kind of great? If young people all over Japan were to turn bad, like those lemmings. One after another, all of them would end up on the bad side. That would be really interesting," she said and laughed to herself again, but maybe my response had been too vague, because then she got quiet. I lay on my back and started rereading Kafka's *The Castle* for the umpteenth time. In the distance I heard the sound of sudden brakes, followed by the blare of a car horn. Sayuko narrowed her eyes as if she were nearsighted, and following her gaze, I could see the moon from the window. Not quite full, but it was shining big, bright, and magnificent, as if flaunting its presence. She often narrowed her eyes like that when she looked at the moon. She said that, on the first night after being abandoned when she was pregnant, the beauty of the full moon hovering in the sky had made her feel miserable.

"Close the curtain, will you?"

I closed it and pressed my body next to hers. She was absently smoking a cigarette; her entire body seemed drained of energy. With her left hand, probably unconsciously, she was touching her own body like a caress, as if just testing it out. I thought to myself that we shouldn't have had sex after all.

"When I look at you, sometimes it gives me the creeps," she said.

I didn't say anything.

"You look like you've lost a lot of weight. I mean, you've been doing all this weird stuff. But . . . I guess that makes you feel better. I'd probably freak out if you ever actually showed signs of life. Strange to say, but . . ."

It was too early to go to sleep, but I closed my eyes. The next day, she would tell me about the terrible nightmare she'd had.

3

I hadn't been in my taxi for a while, and the smell inside was nauseating. Every time I get into it, I think to myself that this is the wrong job for me, since I don't like cars in the first place. Then again, what does it matter anyway? I've never come across a job I've been suited for, and even if I managed to figure out what that was, I'd never be able to earn a living.

At the rotary in front of Ikebukuro Station's West Exit, there were already more than thirty taxis queued up. I should have found another spot, but I had already stopped the car so I just stayed put. I lit a cigarette, turning off the air conditioner, which was blowing that unpleasant smell, and opening the window. The other drivers—middle-aged men—were outside drinking coffee and looking in my direction. Before I could think of what to do, one of them had called out to me, "What happened to your face?" I didn't say anything, but he still wore an anxious expression. "I hope it wasn't a taxi robbery. There've been a lot of those lately. Guys with no money steal from the ones who don't have any money either. But you look pretty banged up. Did you get into a fight or something?"

Just because we were both taxi drivers, he thought that gave him the right to talk to me. I didn't understand his taking such an interest in someone else's business. When it came to dealing with other people, sustaining ongoing relationships just didn't come easily for me. With Sayuko, even, it was more from inertia than anything else that our relationship had managed to go on this long.

I turned the steering wheel as I stepped on the gas and drove off without replying. I felt guilty, thinking about how surprised he looked. But then again, wasn't I wrong to feel like it was my fault? If I was going to feel guilty, then I should have just answered him in the first place.

IT MAY HAVE been my lack of enthusiasm, but by nighttime, I still hadn't picked up any fares. Just as I was about to turn the corner at the post office, I caught sight of a middle-aged man with his arm raised in my direction, in front of a convenience store on my left. Since I had taken a little time off, this was my first fare in a week. He was drunk. He had been muttering something to himself since before he got in the cab. I was bummed to realize that he was the type who would want to make conversation. I had been subjected to lengthy speeches by passengers like him before, about the economy or politics or whatever the hell they wanted to talk about. After he told me where he was going, he asked how my business was going. I had no excuses to offer. Even on this fare, the meter wouldn't even get to fifteen hundred yen before I reached his destination.

"Oh, you're young . . . I bet you're about the same age as my son . . . "

He began speaking in a friendly tone as he looked at the photo of me posted behind the driver's seat. It had been taken when I first joined the company. He took another look at my taxi license, which had only been taken a short time ago, but my face looked even younger in that photo.

"But . . . isn't that unusual? I think you must be the youngest taxi driver I've ever had. Hmm, I guess young people today don't want to drive a taxi, do they?"

He seemed to expect a response so I grunted vaguely.

"I always assumed that guys who end up doing this have already tried doing various other jobs . . . isn't that right? You're still young, there must be something else you can do, isn't there?"

How depressing that the light had turned red. He seemed like he would be offended if I gave another vague response. I had no choice but to engage with him.

"Yes, well, I'm looking, but there's the recession." These were the first words I had uttered today.

"Right. Of course. Well, you should be commended just for working at all."

His spirits seemed to have been restored.

"My son, you see, he doesn't work, he's too busy with his music. For him it's as if not to follow his passion would be to deny who he is—it's pathetic, like he's desperate or something. And all he does is waste money, buying all kinds of equipment and CDs."

He lit a cigarette, still chattering away.

"When we were his age, we had other things on our mind . . . When I was at university, I ran wild with my friends. You all probably wouldn't understand. Nowadays, there are always all kinds of things happening—one after another—for you to go wild about, isn't that right? But you're all too meek. You're like sheep. And you all seem to be crazy about war, don't you?"

The light turned green, but the car in front of me was remarkably slow to react. Its speed was erratic, and every so often the car seemed like it was being drawn over to the right. Thinking the driver might be drunk, I moved into the left lane.

"Ah, you're all just a flock of sheep. Nothing more

than a self-serving generation, aren't you? Don't you even care about what's going to happen in the end?"

All the cars behind me were following my lead and trying to change lanes. I thought that other car was about to crash into something. I cracked my window; it reeked of alcohol inside the taxi.

"You're all obsessed with your own problems. Well, I don't know about you personally, but that's how the one I've got is, at least. All he wants to do is mope about his own problems, all by himself. That's why he's going to fall flat on his face."

He swayed contentedly to the pop song that was playing on the radio. His eyes were closed, so maybe he would just fall asleep. It would be a drag if he threw up while he was sleeping. As I was watching him in the rearview mirror, he suddenly opened his eyes.

"Hey, what's the matter? What happened to your face? It's all swollen, isn't it?"

Our eyes met in the rearview mirror. "I fell down drinking," I said, and he let out a big laugh. We had arrived at his destination, but he was reeling; I had to help him out of the car.

ON MY WAY back to the garage, I happened to pass that same park and got out of the car. It didn't seem like the guys from the other night were around. I bought a can of coffee from the vending machine and sat on a bench to drink it. On the playground next to the slide, there were two cylindrical pieces of equipment shaped like tunnels. Their configuration wasn't necessarily designed to envelop whoever was inside and block out their surroundings, but they seemed beautiful to me. Or maybe they were made for adults—this foolish idea occurred to me as I crawled inside, as if beckoned there, and lit a cigarette. My hips were in a weird position, but I kind of liked the feel of the cool concrete.

Ever since I had been contacted by the orphanage, I seemed to be going through a phase of progressively worse behavior. A week ago, I learned that my father was still alive at the same time that I found out my mother had died. It was always like this. Just when I thought I had gotten over something, whatever it was would stubbornly reappear in my life. What did it mean to me now to know that my father was alive? My parents—both of whom had vanished from my

life—didn't even exist in memory. I couldn't understand his desire to see me. The mere fact of it, at this
point in time, didn't seem right to me.

After both my parents had left me, I had moved
around from one home to another. I had only faint
memories from that time, but eventually I was taken
in by the family of a distant relative, which I remember
clearly. I don't know how many times I was kicked and
smacked around while I was there. My only hope was
to survive without being beaten, to live without the
fear of death. It would have been childish to focus
my attention on the existence of my real parents, and
there was never a chance to anyway. It wasn't until I
was in the custody of the orphanage that I began to
think about it.

For a while, I was swayed by the idea that if my
parents hadn't abandoned me, I wouldn't have had to
go through what I did. That kind of wishful thinking
was probably just my own weakness, an abstract
notion of parents I didn't remember, now nothing
more than the object of my resentment. But I was
still puzzled by the fact that there were times when
I tried to imagine them. Even though they ultimately

abandoned me, I wondered whether—before that, back when I was born—they had any hopes for me. Like, that I would be a good person, or that I would be successful. If I could have known what they hoped for back then, perhaps I might actually be able to live my life with those aspirations. Thinking there must have been some kind of reason or circumstance, a part of me had probably been trying to hold out for a place where I could return home to, for the time when I ought to have been there. But then, as I grew up and the days and months passed without any contact from my parents, that hope faded away within me. And now it had been more than twenty years.

At this point in time, none of this mattered to me anymore. These days, as long as I am working, I can live my life. I am not unhappy, nor at a disadvantage. And when I do think about what happened in that home, the mere fact that I'd survived to the age of twenty-seven made me think that it wasn't such a big deal. And now, my father's recent appearance didn't evoke the slightest feelings at all. I hadn't bothered to ask the person who called from the orphanage for any further details about him.

The only problem was, I was gradually losing whatever motivation I had. Even just making it through
the day was hard lately. It wasn't that I thought about
killing myself. But I did feel as if I were being drawn
toward death. Obviously it seemed wrong to describe
it as an aspiration, but there was a desire inside me I
couldn't identify. All I knew was that it was distorting
my life.

I emerged from the tunnel, but the scenery was
unchanged. The moon that Sayuko and I had tried
not to see was still shining against the surrounding
clouds, the same way it was last night. I went back to
the car and started the engine. On the radio, a report
about the war was being replayed on the air.

WHEN I GOT back to my apartment, a woman was
lying in front of my door. Her turned-up skirt was probably the work of one of my neighbors. As I got closer, I
could tell it was Sayuko. Other than her, there was no
one who had any reason to be at my apartment.

When I brushed her long hair up out of her face, I
saw that she was quite drunk. Her face was flushed,

and her expression was twisted from her ragged and intermittent breathing. By now I had seen Sayuko like this many times. I picked her up, brought her inside, and put her to bed. The smell of alcohol pervaded the air around her, so I opened the window and laid a wet washcloth on her forehead. She was huffing and puffing violently, like an enormous pump. If this kept up, I would probably need to take her to the hospital. Like me, she detested the hospital.

About two hours later she awoke, while I was watching television I had no interest in and listening to music I didn't care for. In a hoarse voice, she apologized over and over, almost obstinately, for losing her key to the apartment. As I listened to her, I noticed that she was being extra solicitous of me.

"You're not going to ask me why I'm so drunk?"

"Why would I?"

"Wow, that's mean. Don't you care about me at all?" She laughed bitterly as she said this.

"No, that's not it. It's just that I'm no good with snappy comebacks."

"Believe me, I know. Why don't you just kick me out?"

As she was watching me, I lit a cigarette and searched for the right words. The tobacco smoke formed a white stream that gradually lost shape before dissipating completely.

"Why are you staying here at all?"

"I . . . Uh . . . " Whether she was thinking about what to say, or she was put out by my cowardly reply, she tilted her head back and began staring at the ceiling, the way she did when we had sex. "I've told you about my parents before, haven't I?"

"Yes, a few times," I said, but she kept on talking as if she hadn't heard me.

"My mother . . . no matter what my father did to her, she never left him. He had other women, he was violent when he was drunk, he spent all our money— but she still clung to him until the end. I hated my mother. I promised myself I would never be like that. But we can't necessarily keep up with the promises we make to ourselves, you know?"

I nodded with my cigarette in my mouth.

"Until now, there haven't been any decent guys. Even guys with kids, they were just unimaginably worthless. So quick to tell me they love me, like

fools, and then they just disappeared . . . Well, there's
nothing decent about me, either, so I guess they suit
me. Judging by the types I go for, I'm just like the
mother I was so disgusted with."

She laughed as she said this, but she was still
staring up at the ceiling.

"When I stopped feeling things, I was stupid
enough to think I had learned my lesson—that maybe
my body had gone numb so I would stay away from
men. But here I am, dependent on you. Since my
mother died, I feel useless. Really, even I'm surprised
by how I just don't want to do anything. I can't even
muster the courage to kill myself."

"That's inevitable. You worked night and day to earn
the money to pay for your mother's treatment. You're
exhausted. Even though you hated her, you still tried
to save her in the end, didn't you?"

"Is that what you think?" she said. She seemed to
laugh at herself. Her drunken pallor now gave off a
strange radiance. "Caring for her was just a way for
me to get back at her. I was just showing my mother,
*Look, because of you, see how hard your daughter has
to work, day and night? How awful, isn't it? She looks*

*exhausted, doesn't she?* I was pretty persistent in my revenge."

"I doubt that."

"It's true, that's the kind of person I am. My mother . . . she even laid out a futon for my father and whatever woman he brought home. Of course that would make anyone sick, right? I hated her. Not just my mother. That whole family, I really hated them. But the one I hate the most is myself—always a wreck, manipulated like a fool, and such a mess I let the guy who knocked me up get away and lost my baby."

"Stop it," I raised my voice a little. "You're tired, and you're drunk. Go to bed already."

"In the end, when I die, my life will have been just like my parents'. Doesn't that scare you to think about? I hate how much I'm like my mother. I do everything I can to try to change, but instead I end up even more like her."

She looked at me as she fell silent, as if searching for the words and only now realizing she had stopped talking. I had to say something.

"Aw, it's all right. And the ones who hit me weren't

my real parents. They were distant relatives, a married couple who took me in after my parents left."

". . . Right. But in that case, there's still hope for your real parents."

It was as if the black smudges on the wall were talking to me. The wall was damaged and uneven, and if I looked closely, it resembled a man's crestfallen face.

"I'm past the age for thinking about that. But I used to wonder, once in a while. Like when I won an art prize in school, I wondered if my parents were good at drawing. And when my homeroom teacher told me I was introverted, I wondered whether my parents were too. I feel like, by analyzing myself, instead I start to see my parents."

"Right—you need to find out more about your parents."

"But what happens when I find out? Look, I've asked those questions myself. But nobody from the orphanage has told me anything anyway. And . . . well, that pretty much makes me think there's nothing good about them. When I was in junior high, someone from the orphanage tried to tell me, but I didn't want to hear about my parents back then. I was annoyed, but really, none of this crap matters at this point, does it? Parents are parents, and children are children. It makes no difference."

Sayuko looked as though she might say something in response, but she was silent. The television was still on; there was a news report about a random murder. The killer was jaded about life and decided to kill someone. Next, there had been another murder for insurance money; then they showed a photograph of a child who had been run over by a truck driver who was driving drunk. A teacher had struck a student, and the student had hit the teacher back. I lit a cigarette and inhaled deeply.

"You have your parents, and I have mine." Before I knew it, I had started speaking again. "But it makes no difference. There must be a part of you that is passed down from them, but we think for ourselves and— it may sound obvious, but—our character depends on our environment, and we started out as different people. You're too anxious about that kind of thing, whether it's in your blood or your DNA. It does no good just to blame your parents."

She seemed slightly bewildered by me talking this way. I felt sheepish.

"I'm sure you're right, but it drives me crazy. Thinking about even a drop of my mother's or that asshole's blood in my veins. And I hate that there isn't a damn thing I can do about it. It's like I've got a lump in the pit of my stomach. As if their genes are living inside of me. Like I'm marked by them and can't help taking on their qualities. I know that's just in my head, but their blood really is in my veins, isn't it? Physiologically, I can't stand it."

I knew just what she meant. Yet still, I wondered why I had pushed the conversation to the point where it hurt her.

"It seems like I'm getting worse and worse—it's scary. It's hard to describe, but I feel like there's someone behind me, pushing me along. I'm resisting but—how can I put it?—maybe my resistance only makes things worse? Oh, forget it . . . I'm sick of it."

I lit another cigarette, and imagined there was a lump in the pit of my own stomach. It felt creepy to think about a complete stranger's information being embedded within me. I wondered if there were minute twitches, like threads strung throughout my body, that exerted an imperceptible influence on me, on my decisions and my actions.

Suddenly, I felt depressed about the prospect of waking up the next day. The relentless progression of one day after another seemed to engulf me like heavy smoke. But since this happened all the time, I was familiar enough with ways to regulate my mood swings. I opened the pages of *The Castle* once more. I went around in circles, as if burying myself in the words of the unfathomable ending.

4

I threw the can of coffee I had been drinking out the window. This apartment was on the fourth floor, so it was a pretty good distance from the ground. Whenever I did this, I always felt a sense of tension. My fingers seemed to stiffen with numbness, and they were slippery with perspiration where they came in contact with the can. I would grow anxious. My heartbeat would gradually start to race, and it almost felt as though the effort to stop what I was doing took over in my fingers before the idea even reached my consciousness. Yet, as if in rebellion, my hand would let go. I couldn't tell whether that had actually been my intention or if I were merely resisting an urge. I regretted it after I let go, and yet I was suffused with a distinct sense of liberation. My chest was thumping as I watched to make sure the can hit the ground. The sensation of going from tension to liberation, coupled with a renewed anxiety, had caused sweat to break out on the nape of my neck and my breath to quicken as if harried. The can was no longer in my power. Its trajectory may have been by my own action, but at this point it was outside of my control. Everything was moving so slowly. When would it hit the ground below? It should have crashed by now. What was taking so long? Suddenly a hard high-pitched sound echoed, and I felt a weight in my chest as if my heart had been struck. The can bounced high off the ground and, after flying through the air a second time, it rolled away, now just another piece of trash on the ground. That had taken even longer than I expected. Now I wanted to drop something heavier, something that would offer more resistance.

It may sound strange, but I've always enjoyed dropping things. Well, it's not so much that I enjoy it, but rather that it was something I did, over and over—that seems more accurate. The orphanage that had taken me in as a child was on a low hill, and if I walked a short distance from the back door, there was a cliff about twenty meters high. In front of it was a high green fence that was supposed to keep us away from the cliff. But my young hands were still small, and I dropped all sorts of things off the cliff by reaching through the fence. Bottles, rocks, cans, scraps of metal, sand . . . but what excited me the most was when I dropped lizards or other creatures. Grasping a lizard that had already lost its tail or an unsuspecting frog, I would thrust my arm through the fence and suddenly let go. This living thing would fall, and although it wasn't dead yet, surely it would be a few seconds later. Watching this happen always evoked anxiety, but for some reason, I found solace in that anxiety. In the midst of my agitated emotions, I felt a clear awakening as nostalgia tinged with sweetness spread within me. When I did this, I would also be thinking about "them"—the ones who had tormented me. This

habit was persistent in its cruelty; it was almost as if
by what I was doing to those lizards now, I was vali-
dating what had been done to me in the past, as if I
were exploring the true nature of it. Say someone hit
me. The moment that blow was released, it could no
longer be taken back. And whether that blow would
kill me or whether I would survive cannot be decided
by him, nor by me. The relationship between the force
of the blow and my resilience cannot be determined
by anyone. The lizard would plummet. No matter how
much the lizard struggled in the air, the result would
be the same. I had already let go of it. All that was
left was however much time passed before it crashed
to the ground. This was violence—overwhelming
violence, without any recourse. And that crippling
passivity . . . Leaving me—now the perpetrator—with
a thumping chest, anxiety, and regret. But they did
not feel that way toward me. Then again, perhaps they
had felt a sense of liberation.

But I think there was actually something else
behind this act, beyond my exploration of the nature
of violence. Within this broader phenomenon that was
driving me, whatever this other force was seemed to

pierce the core of my being. It was indistinct, uniden-
tifiable—just like the thing that had been just beyond
my grasp when those guys on the bikes were kicking
me. This sensation and the validation of the violence
itself were intertwined, and something seemed as
though it was trying to take shape.

Realizing I was hungry, I opened the refrigerator,
but there was nothing to eat. Judging by the faint whiff
of alcohol that lingered in the apartment, I assumed
that Sayuko had gone back out again. I wished she
were here now, though I wasn't sure for what purpose.
But that was just my ego, since my desire to have her
here wasn't actually about her specifically. It was more
of a fleeting impulse; I would be lying to myself if I
said there was anything I wanted to talk to her about.
People can't live without a certain amount of self-
indulgence—I think I remember one of my teachers in
high school saying something like that. But I couldn't
allow myself to drag anybody else into the life of mis-
fortune I expected to lead.

I took the day off from work again, despite not
having anything I needed to get done. This was never
a good sign. Driving a cab is not a job where the work

makes you forget the time. I should have looked for the kind of job that I could lose myself in, maybe repetitive menial labor like factory work with a quota system. The day would pass before I realized it, I would be tired, I would sleep, then back to work, and before I knew it more time would pass. I wondered how much better I would feel, if I could occupy the hours of my life that way. I didn't care whether it was boring or interesting work. I think I'd be fine as long as I could just edge toward the prospect of letting go, with the possibility of escaping my depressive tendencies.

I LEFT THE apartment and went to a grungy restaurant where I ate a heaping mess of fried rice off a dirty plate. I drank a beer, and before I knew it, an hour had gone by. During that time, I had been muttering to myself, enough so that the married couple who run the restaurant were now checking me out. Definitely another bad sign. When I left the restaurant, it was so late that there was hardly anyone on the street. Every so often the light from a passing bicycle shone on me before receding into the distance. I heard several car horns—they might have been directed at me. *I feel drunk*, I thought to myself, even though I knew very well that I wasn't actually drunk.

There was a toad smushed on the asphalt, lying on its back with both its arms raised as if in a full-body expression of joy. I walked two or three steps farther, and there was a lightly soiled white glove, its limp index finger pointing to the right. I cocked my head, and took a right turn down a narrow street. A small dog that was tied up started barking at me like mad, as if it were really going to do me harm. If I could melt away into the darkness, I thought to myself, that might make me happy. I didn't know what happiness was, but I figured I might at least be at ease. I looked up at a ten-story apartment building and considered throwing something off the top of it. My heart skipped a little at this childish idea. I bought a can of coffee from a vending machine and took the stairs up, rather than the elevator. The steady echo of my footsteps made this act into a kind of ritual. The air was cool—maybe the concrete had absorbed the heat. Whenever I reached a landing, the gently blowing breeze seemed to dry my sweat a little more.

On the landing before the highest floor, the wind felt stronger. From there I looked down, holding the unopened can between my thumb and index finger. At that point, I let go. Immediately, my insides were awhirl with an anxiety that felt like regret. With its contents intact, the can fell with terrific speed. It was unbearable to imagine that the can might feel fear as it plummeted. Perhaps this angst was what linked me—the perpetrator—to the can. I pondered whether this sense of affinity for the can might be a form of affection. In the stillness of the night air, the sound of a dull shattering reverberated. The coffee inside the can spurted out like blood, spattering all around as it rolled, traveling farther than I had expected. I wanted to drop something else. The edge of the concrete wall that protected the landing arced gently toward the exterior. I wondered about this design as I approached it again, noticing how well the curvature fit my body. I rested my belly on it, entrusting my weight to the curve as I leaned my torso out over it. I thought I saw something in the beyond, something other than the ground that seemed so far away. My knees buckled and I felt weak, but in a way, this sensation also seemed comfortable to me. In the midst of falling, would my awareness reach a certain end point? By dropping myself, I would become both the perpetrator and the victim. What would I see on the other side of the fear and anxiety? I felt like I could do what I had to do, if I found out just what that was. In the time before I collided with the ground, at the moment when I knew there was absolutely no turning back, would my body feel the stab of devastating regret? As I fell, would my hands grasp at the air? Would my somersaulting body struggle to stabilize itself, despite that fact that doing so would be of no use? As I anticipated the certainty of the approaching impact, I would resent everything and everyone. I would thrash around, trying to slip away from my existence that was absolutely, inescapably, only moments away from certain death. Experiencing that complete and overwhelming force would bring me closer to my core—and I am convinced that, within that core, my true self would be revealed. But what was it that made me think so? It didn't matter. The opportunity to actually experience it was right before my eyes. Right now, if I just leaned my body forward, as if I were going to spin around a horizontal bar, I would fall down below. I would fall, tumbling down—out of this life, out of this world . . . Little by little, I tipped my center of gravity forward. *Just do it already*, I thought as if teasing myself. My heart was pounding, my body dripping with sweat. It wasn't so bad. This agitation, this anxiety—it felt like my own flesh and blood. Along the edge of the wall, beetles were crawling around, their bodies gleaming green. When I leaned out, I saw that streaks of grime, like brown rust, had formed a branched pattern on the outer wall. A chill seeped from within the concrete, its surface insistently rough to the touch, a sensation I savored. My body was tilting forward. I felt like a seesaw, balancing myself. A cigarette slipped out of my shirt pocket; it fell with such speed that I found it difficult to follow its descent. As if that had been a cue, one after another, the rest of the cigarettes begin to fall, like a mass suicide. They looked like a string of white arrows, enticing me. When my slowly shifting center of gravity had gone beyond a certain point, my body slid forward, irrespective of my own will, and I felt a sudden pull downward. I was caught by an overwhelming force. I put my strength into both arms, and at the same time, my back and legs sprang to life. After flailing around in the air like I was going to burst, I had a slight ringing in my ears and my vision was blurry. I felt a stab of pain like a stitch in my right side. There I was, lying on the landing of the stairs, but I didn't know what had happened. When I looked at the gentle arc of the wall in front of me, my entire body went weak, and I suppressed my trembling as well as a shriek that I felt welling up inside me. My chest was tight with shortened breath from the shock of what I had just attempted to do. No, my actions had not been unintentional. I very clearly remembered my stream of thoughts as I had been trying to drop myself over the edge. But I didn't know what it meant. Why had I done such a thing? I knew the reason—I was well aware of it. Perhaps the fact that I lay here now, unscathed, was what went against my own will. I had no strength in my legs, I couldn't stand up. I reached for a cigarette in order to calm myself down, but there were none left in my shirt pocket. It was difficult to go down the stairs; for the first five flights or so, I could only move in a crouched position.

When I set foot on the ground, I felt dizzy from such an overpowering sense of stability and expansiveness, and I had to sit down again. About ten meters away, in a conspicuously vacant parking lot, I found the can I had dropped. Like another version of me, it was horribly crushed and had made a disgusting mess all around it.

5

For a few years, until the age of eight, I spent most of my time lying in a narrow room made up of nailed-together storm shutters, on the outermost end of a corner apartment on the first floor of a building. When I look back over my life, unfortunately I don't have any particularly strong or clear memories from the time I was taken in by this family. Why "they" had decided to take me in was not for me to understand as a small child. Whether they received money periodically or it was an arbitrary decision—to this day, I still don't know.

They were distant relatives of mine, a married couple with a newborn of their own, and they were wary of me doing harm to their infant. The door to their rooms was secured from the outside with a simply fashioned lock. I was just a child, I couldn't help but want someone to take care of me. I doubt it would have mattered to me whether it were by my real parents or someone else. In the beginning, they found my screams when they beat me funny, and they laughed at me. I preferred being hit to being kicked. I could still feel a kind of nearness to whomever was beating me—it was the closest thing I got to intimacy.

Their baby was beautiful. He had clear eyes and fat lips that were always glossy and red. When the baby would cry or become hysterical, they would strike me. "It stands to reason that we would beat you when the baby is crying!" I couldn't understand what they meant. But I was very young then, and who was I to question their logic? I thought that was how the world was. I just accepted my place in it.

One day after the baby learned to stand, he

happened to come into my room. Our eyes met, and for a few seconds we just stared at each other. I smiled at how beautiful he was, but the baby's face turned red and he let out a terrible cry. It might have been the traces of blood caked on my swollen face that he thought were simply terrifying. The baby was beautiful even when he was crying, and his skin was so soft and clean that I hesitated to touch him. That was when I first understood that undeniable differences existed among human beings. I felt the obvious distance that separated me from the baby—our destiny was stamped upon each of us. I could do nothing but stare at him. I knew this difference was beyond my control, that it was something I could not change. The man would raise his fist to strike me. I would clench my teeth and bear up with my whole being as I waited for this predetermined event. My body was ruled by fear. It was my fear that imagined and anticipated the violence, enabling me to exceed my level of tolerance. The fist approached, as surely determined as the crash into the ground that follows a fall. I simply waited for it . . . Violence became easier to commit the more one wielded it. I no longer hoped to escape—what I longed for was a respite. An existence in which, for even just a brief span of time, I would not be attacked, where I could sleep peacefully.

It was not long before their violence escalated. It wasn't that they devised an elaborate plan against me; they just put more effort into their actions. The man primarily struck me with his own hands and feet; the woman occasionally also used to an iron or a pipe from the vacuum cleaner. What I found most unbearable was the look of boredom on their faces when they let loose on me. They seemed weary and annoyed as they struck and kicked me; they had no particular hatred or fury, or even curiosity. I didn't cry at the pain—not because I was tough; it was more like I had forgotten to—but their expressions were what ultimately made me weep.

What evoked their violence toward me in the first place? I had given some thought to this question. The conclusion my young self arrived at was that they were not me—they were others. If they had considered what it felt like to be me, they wouldn't treat me this way. I couldn't help but wonder what any existence outside of myself was like, or what kinds of things others were capable of doing. Each time they kicked me, I began to murmur inside my head, "They're not me."

A burst of violence left a hole in the wall, which was thin to begin with. It was only one day before it was filled in, but through that opening, I managed to steal a glimpse at the television. It was a travel show with a couple of entertainers, a man and a woman. The man acted out some joke and the woman laughed, then the woman made some kind of request and the man happily obliged. I realized that, out there, a whole world existed that had nothing to do with me. Far away, there were people who had nothing to do with me, who were experiencing their own form of happiness. Each time they laughed, I felt angry. There was nowhere for this anger to go. It was a wriggling sensation that accumulated within me like a swirling eddy. A woman in a bathing suit advertised for iced coffee, a man wearing a suit was giving a detailed explanation of the capabilities of a camera. I hated this world that smiled and passed by, without any concern for me—hated it with all my energy, hated it enough that it consumed me. It was around this time that the look in my eyes hardened—my eyes narrowed, the corners turned up ever so slightly—but still to the point where it was noticeable. That angled gaze that was first reflected back in the mirror is still seared in my mind. This was also around the time when I became mute. At first I refused to speak, but before long, when I tried to open my mouth, I would feel suffocated, like it was hard to breathe.

The violence gradually became less frequent, and in due time I was merely neglected. They had begun to shun me, like an animal who did nothing more than eat and shit. I experienced for the first time the excruciating pain that accompanies severe hunger, along with a raging fever that took over my body, refusing to break. The decline in my physical strength brought on a decline in my consciousness. For the first time I also came to understand that thought itself requires energy.

One day, there came a turning point. I was seated at their dining table, a plate of curry rice set before me. I was so weakened that I hadn't been able to stand; I had been dragged like a doll and forced to sit there. "Eat this," the man said. "Eat this and then you're going away."

Someone else had brought up the idea of taking me in, and the couple had jumped at the chance to be rid of me. They intended to fatten me up and nurse my wounds in order to conceal their violence and neglect. My mouth was watering, but I was unable to eat. My stomach churned in pain, and I vomited in front of them. They were furious, and they hit me for the first time in a while. Had I been able to eat that plate of food back then, perhaps a different life would have awaited me. Of course, there was also the possibility that an even crueler fate lay in store. But it doesn't matter; I wouldn't have been able to eat anything in any case.

From the time after that, I have only scattered memories. Or, more precisely, I remember, but my memories are not accompanied by images. It seemed as though my body lost its shape and was replaced with a dark haze. My will to live—the basic desires to sleep or drink— emerged vaguely from that haze, only to be extinguished by the pain from each successive blow. I had been transformed into a mass of sensation. During that time, it occurred to me that this might be the true form of a human being. I felt as though the mass I had become was the root of existence.

## 6

When I opened my eyes, my heart was pounding and Sayuko was shaking me by the shoulders. She stared at me dubiously and kept asking if I was okay. I shivered in a cold sweat; it was difficult to breathe. "You were having a nightmare," she said. "You usually quiet down when I shake you by the shoulders, but this time you woke up."

She smiled and her dimples showed in her cheeks. Seeing them suddenly made me feel depressed.

The dream from a moment ago remained clear in my mind—I remembered every detail. A huge dark mass had been trying to crush my body. But it wasn't fear that I'd felt; I had been laughing as I was being crushed. Sleep with me, I said, and Sayuko nodded calmly.

While we were having sex, I couldn't shake the thought that this act was totally absurd. Despite her lack of sensation, Sayuko ran her fingertips through my hair, which gave me some solace. I was filled with foreboding at the thought that a person like me was alive. I checked myself before my mind headed off in this direction; nothing good ever came of it.

The next thing I knew, I had stopped moving. I felt a ripple of premonition; still holding her in my arms, I couldn't go on any longer. When she asked me what was wrong, I couldn't find the right words. After a little while, she let out a sigh loud enough for me to hear.

"It gets boring, doesn't it?" Sayuko said with a defensive iciness in her voice.

"That's not it."

"So then why did you give up?"

"I didn't give up. I don't know why, I can't really say."

"Because it's boring, isn't it? Sleeping with a woman like me. You'd be better off not bothering, wouldn't you? There's no reason to be sentimental—just be objective."

"That's not it, I just, I feel bad about how I treat you."

"What?"

"Because you do so much for me, and I just want to sleep with you, right? Even though you don't get any pleasure from it."

"You let me stay in this apartment, don't you?"

"That's not what I mean. Other than that, I don't do anything for you."

She was looking at me curiously. "What happened all of a sudden? Are you worried about me?"

"Probably. But . . . that's not all it's about. I'm sick of it."

"Sick of sleeping with someone like me?"

"Not that."

"So what then?"

"Just of myself, of being totally useless, like an insect waiting to die. I'm good for nothing. Aren't I right?"

She parted her lips, but seemed unable to fathom

the meaning of what I had said. The moonlight shone faintly through a gap in the curtains, casting a pale shadow on Sayuko's gaunt cheek. I don't know why, but for some reason the sight of it made me choke up. Even though we were in the midst of a quarrel, I couldn't take my eyes off of her.

"Fine. If you want to end things with me."

"No, that's not what I mean, but for now—what am I trying to say?—I still want to be with you. It's just . . . I want things to be different from how they always are, at least for today. That sounds stupid—it probably makes you sick," I said, and for the first time, she laughed.

"Ah, you're in a bad way. And now, in this state, you're stuck having to rely on someone like me."

"You're not the kind of person you think you are."

"It's okay, you don't have to coddle me."

I tried to reply, but again I couldn't find the right words to say.

SAYUKO SAID SHE was going out to get some things and I saw her to the door, but then I was feeling pretty lazy so I got back into bed and slept. I figured I'd take the day off from work again. I knew I would get fired if I kept this up, but I couldn't muster any sense of urgency. I turned on the television, but nothing stuck in my brain. The apartment felt claustrophobic; I felt a strange oppressiveness throughout my entire body.

A mosquito that had come in through the window flew at me relentlessly. I pitied its sorry existence, this creature that announces itself by buzzing whenever it approaches its target. I blocked its way with my hand, but it managed to get around. When it went behind the television, I even got up to follow it. It settled on the wall and I struck it with my hand; it got away and I tried to catch it in the air. I knew I was being ridiculous, but I didn't care. I saw it land on the table, and I covered it with a glass. For a moment the mosquito flew up fiercely, but then it just drifted within the confined space, seemingly confused by the situation in which it found itself. It could no longer escape. Maybe I was now like a god to it. I could do whatever I liked with it.

≈

I WENT OUTSIDE. The sultry heat was stifling. I cast an eye over my surroundings as I walked along, thinking I would try to distract myself from my deteriorating mood. The intense moonlight formed a circle behind the thin and uneven cloud cover, its pale bluish-gray color gleaming hazily. I came out of a narrow passageway between brick condominiums, turned alongside a row house, and came out onto a wide road with cars on it. As I turned my attention to the light from a convenience store, a tall woman came out with a crying child in tow. She was trying to soothe the child, but he seemed inconsolable, and his cries were rising in intensity. With every step, the child's shoes made a high and comical sound, like a whistle. I felt an affinity for these two, and I stopped where I was to light a cigarette. Just then, the woman struck the child. It was as if an intense light had flashed before my eyes, momentarily blinding me. A delayed numbness spread down both my arms, and my heart had gradually begun to race. The sound of the child's shoes echoed in my mind. My head ached, and I wanted to get away from there, but I couldn't bring myself to leave. Yet right in front of me was the figure of this woman, gently soothing the child. Everything about the scene from before I had stopped in my tracks remained the same. The woman continued to console the child, and the child kept crying. Could it have been my imagination? I could have sworn that the woman had struck the child, but in fact maybe she hadn't? I didn't know, but I gave up thinking about it and left the scene.

I turned the corner of an old apartment building and headed into an alley where, on the asphalt illuminated by the streetlight, there was a huge number of shriveled-up earthworm carcasses, so many that there wasn't anywhere to walk. Not wanting to turn back, I had no choice but to step on them. But the unmistakable soft sensation nauseated me. Four or five young guys were walking nearby, their laughter exaggerated. As they came closer, I got nervous, practically holding my breath as I passed them. At that moment, the image of the woman striking the child flashed in my mind, and I assumed that must have been the cause of my stress.

When I came out onto the road alongside the river, something about the faint current partially obscured by the barrier fence made me stop in my tracks. I don't know what bothered me about it, but the idea of falling to one's death in those depths gave me a bad vibe. On the riverbank there was the wreckage of a bicycle, broken in two and covered in dried gray mud, as if it had been forced down into the earth. I could not tear my eyes away from the sight of that gray mass that used to be a bicycle. As I was beginning to feel more relaxed, I felt a warmth that seemed to permeate my entire body. I realized that I hoped I would end up like that wrecked bicycle—I would be broken in two, shriveled up, buried in the mud. I imagined the cool sensation of the earth as each tiny coarse grain penetrated inside me, trying to erode me. I shuddered in an attempt to shake off the image, and I left the scene behind me.

Still without an objective, I had no choice but to keep walking. As I moved along, I thought about death. At first, like a game, I tried to imagine what might happen if I were to die now. My heartbeat became violent; it was so impossibly fierce, it seemed to bash about my insides. It gave me the creeps, and I stopped walking. My anxiety seemed to have a will of its own, and I couldn't stop it from spreading through me. Did I wish for my own death? Was that the effect of being caught up in all of these strange behaviors? It might seem like that was the case, but I had the feeling it wasn't. Nevertheless, I couldn't help but think that death might be near at hand. My heart still pounding, I concentrated my attention on the sound of a railroad crossing that I could hear in the distance. I thought I might die soon. With a steady rhythm, the railroad crossing called to me, and I felt myself drawn by it as if I were a puppet on a string. It wasn't so bad. I must really be vulnerable to be so obviously open to suggestion. Suddenly the world surrounding me seemed enormous. The land that spread out into fields, the sky covered in gray clouds, the road, even the air that was invisible to the eye—everything seemed to possess an immense and overwhelming presence. Cast within such a vastness, my own existence was futile, utterly powerless—even if I devoted my entire being I couldn't leave even the slightest mark on this world. The world was mighty, it expanded coldly—it existed without seeing me. I might as well die. Even if I gave my life, the world would still not take notice of me. Death had the same value as everything else within this cruel vastness spread before me—no value at all. There were no second chances. My heart ached, I had no strength in my legs—I couldn't move. And yet, despite this terrifying feeling, I still couldn't quite grasp its significance; I never caught up with myself. The railroad crossing continued to chime its steadfast rhythm. It felt as though another me was trying to free himself from the version of me who was frightened by this. I was a part of the cold world. And my death wouldn't make any difference. I walked in the direction of the sound, but I could no longer hear it, and the green fence, the ground, the clouds, the row of utility poles—everything started to take back its ordinary color. Once again I found myself in front of the wide road. I was lightheaded and, unable to stand, I sank to the ground. Several pedestrians passed by me. Where was I? I wondered, and I looked around for a moment. Some people looked down on me and frowned as they walked past, others purposely avoided looking my way. I wondered what they were doing in a place like this. I looked up, and I could see a billboard for a personal finance loan I had never heard of. I felt another wave of dizziness and thought I might throw up. There was something familiar about this feeling. As if my physiological frenzy was pumping the blood through my veins, and my own contours seemed like they were gradually becoming more distinct.

The balance in my bank account was dwindling since I had been taking off from work. I thought about what would happen if I stayed on this slippery downward slope, just kept borrowing money, without any limits. That salaryman that Sayuko had talked about, had he ultimately found something? She said he seemed content—had he reached a place where he was satisfied? Strangely, out of nowhere, I thought of my father. The image of this man—a complete stranger to me—busily borrowing money flitted through my mind. It made me uncomfortable. I recalled my earlier belief that as long as I was a respectable person then my parents could have been respectable too. It was paradoxical, a strange kind of logic. My lips went slack at the thought. It seemed reasonable to me. I knew it didn't really matter, but I chose to believe it anyway.

On my way home, I tried to think about something that would make me feel better, but I got back to my apartment before I could come up with anything. The glass with the mosquito inside was still on top of the table. I set it free, and it bit me more than once. I had no choice but to swat it with my hand. When I saw its corpse clinging to my chest, for some reason it made me angry and I slapped it again. Even when I saw the completely smushed body, it still wasn't enough for me, and I whacked my chest over and over again until it hurt. Reduced to dust, what was left of the mosquito fell to the floor.

7

I got a call from the hospital saying that Sayuko had been injured, so I hailed a taxi. I tried to imagine how she could have ended up drunk in a club and have fallen down the stairs when she'd originally gone out to pick up some things at the store, but I knew that it was entirely plausible. For a heavy drinker like her, it was difficult to stop. When she had asked me why she shouldn't keep drinking, why she should lead a reasonable life, I hadn't been able to give her a good reason.

Visiting hours were over, but I gave Sayuko's name and was allowed into her hospital room. She was in the bed closest to the door in a six-person room divided by curtains. Sayuko's right shoulder and right leg were in slings, and when she saw me, she let go of the magazine she was reading. "Are you all right?" I asked, but I could tell that, in more ways than one, she was not.

"I'm sorry."

"There's no need to apologize. You're lucky you got off light, aren't you?"

Although I had seen her without makeup countless times, I was surprised by her pale, dispirited expression. Her hair was a mess, and her body reeked of alcohol. I had never seen her so weakened, so unresisting. I averted my gaze and would have liked to smoke a cigarette, but I remembered there was no smoking in the hospital. Blankly, she watched my every move.

"If I had gone head-first, I probably would have died, but it's like I was unconsciously protecting myself. Like an idiot."

"Stop that," I said.

She hung her head, her shoulders seeming to tremble from strain. Her breathing was unsteady. My throat tightened with increasing pressure, as if her distress were contagious.

"I was so scared. This was the second time I fell down the stairs . . . When I was pregnant, I was pushed down the stairs . . . The baby's father got angry about something stupid—he was the one who did it. When I fell this time, I had a flashback."

She exhaled deeply.

"In the ambulance, I found out that the baby and I were both okay. I wasn't too far along yet, but the doctor told me it was a miracle. But the baby was stillborn anyway . . . Poor thing. It was saved by a miracle, only to die in the end . . . You know, how could someone use that much force against something that's so weak? I don't think I'll ever forget the feeling of his hands on my back. That's what was so scary—it seemed like it was happening all over again."

Her head still hung down, she didn't look up.

"When someone uses force, they always use it against someone who is weaker than they are," I said.

"They know they'll win, which is why they do it. It's cowardly."

". . . I guess so. I'm sorry. Always talking about myself."

"Hm? Oh . . . It's okay. Don't worry about it."

The white bedcover was finely creased and twisted. The creases were tinged with shadow, and they were now sharply outlined, like they were trying to form the shape of various faces. Every time Sayuko shifted, the faces would contort in strange laughter. I averted my gaze.

"Do you have insurance?"

I thought I would change the subject, but I immediately regretted asking something so impersonal. She gently shook her head.

"Really? Well, it'll be all right. Don't worry about it."

"I can't afford not to worry. I'm the idiot who did this to myself. One way or another, I'll figure it out on my own."

"One way or another—how are you going to figure it out?"

"If she is so inclined, a woman can make money quickly, can't she? Well, I guess a man can, too."

She tried to laugh, but she didn't have the strength, and it came out sounding like a sigh.

"It's okay, I have money," I said. "You can use whatever's in my account, if you need to. I don't have any use for it anyway. Don't be stubborn, or I'll just pay for it myself."

"Aren't you almost out of money?"

"I can manage. Really, it'll be all right. Not the way you meant, but if I were so inclined, I could manage to work it out somehow," I said.

She frowned for a moment. "You seem a little desperate lately. I mean, there's no reason to do that kind of thing for me, is there? And I'm not just talking about this—this giving away all your money. It's like you're all worked up. It's kind of creepy."

"You're the one with the problem right now. The drinking . . . You really should lighten up."

"Yeah . . . but I know I'm not going to quit. I'm sure I'll screw up again somehow, like the idiot I am."

The curtain next to us moved slightly, as if someone were there. It might have been my imagination, but I felt as though everyone else in the hospital room was listening closely to our conversation. Must be pretty

". . . Bring me a book. You read a lot, don't you? I could die of boredom here."

"All the books I have are depressing."

"So why do you read them?"

"I don't really know," I said, laughing softly. "I feel like they save me. They get me thinking about things, even if it's just that I'm not the only person who thinks it's hard to get around in this world."

"Hmm . . . yeah, I don't really know if that's the kind of book I want to read right now, but bring one anyway. And a change of clothes, I guess . . . Whatever."

After the nurse's second request, I left the hospital room. Since it seemed that Sayuko still wanted to talk about things, I decided to come back again the next day. The nurse gave me bits of random advice about Sayuko. She said she hadn't looked up Sayuko's insurance situation, but that Sayuko's body was in really bad shape from the alcohol. When they'd brought her in, Sayuko's condition had been strange—the nurse went on and on in her empathetic tone. I wanted to understand the nurse's good intentions, but I scuttled out of the hospital.

BACK AT MY apartment, I drank for many hours. I had known for a while where Sayuko hid her whiskey. It seemed unlikely I could drink so much in one day, but I just kept filling my glass and drinking it down. I knew full well that, even if I finished this off, she would just get another bottle and start drinking again.

8

I took the train and got off at a small station where the rapid-transit doesn't stop. The building that houses the station looked old and run-down, but plenty of people used it—it was difficult even to walk along the narrow passages. The downtown area appeared unchanged since I came here eight years ago after graduating from high school. Beside the derelict shopping district with its conspicuously shuttered businesses stood a row of garish condominiums, whose presence casually implied that everything was fine.

I could still see the orphanage from the exit of the station, could just make it out through a gap between the condos, on its perch atop a small hill. I used to be ashamed of the building's prominent position. I felt as if we were on display for all of the people downtown.

I could not be more grateful to this institution. I had the feeling I was biting the hand that had fed me by coming here, and for a moment, I was unable to move. But the head of the orphanage was the only person I had ever been able to trust. Otherwise, I just got by, relying on my own self.

I hailed a taxi and gave the name of the building. The driver took one look at me; his expression seemed to say that he had me all figured out. But that might just have been my paranoid tendencies. It was embarrassing that I still hadn't outgrown those kinds of feelings. He asked what I did for a living, and I replied that I was a taxi driver, like him. He nodded deeply. "It's a good job, if I do say so myself," he said. "The pay is low, but there's no need for any calculating or mercenary behavior. No competition to speak of—you know what I mean? Mostly just turf wars."

As I looked at his smiling face, I felt myself starting to relax. I'd never been able to put a customer at ease that way.

A MIDDLE-AGED WOMAN I had never seen before was the one who led me inside. "Mr. Yamane has been expecting you," she said, greeting me with a wide smile. I had seen that kind of smile many times before, though—conveying absolute reassurance, because that was the only thing the bearer had to offer.

From a jungle gym bearing the name of the corporation that had donated it, a boy in short pants was watching me. There were two girls in the sandbox, and at a distance away near the fence, a boy in a white T-shirt was crossing and uncrossing his arms below the elbow, repeating the same movement over and over. The boy in shorts called out in a loud voice, "Good morning!" The boy near the fence who had been moving his arms around glanced over with a shameful look on his face. I felt as if I knew just what he was thinking.

When I had lived here, there was a similarly amiable boy. I don't remember his actual name, but everyone had called him Toku. Whenever someone from the outside arrived he would greet them, and he would eagerly respond to any of their questions. It wasn't a calculation on his part because he wanted to be adopted; now that I think about it, it seems to me he was motivated by pride, that he wanted to show that even in an orphanage he was still able to greet people so cheerfully. He paid attention to my habit of dropping things, and on occasion he forcibly stopped me. "That's just what they expect," he would say, as if he were trying to convince himself, too. "For miserable situations to beget miserable people. I'm not buying into that kind of formulation." (Sometimes he had a strange way of putting things.) "If you do, you're just playing into their hands."

Who had he meant, who were "they"? Probably the world at large. I wondered where Toku was now, and what he was doing. And if he saw me, what would he think? What would he say to me?

MR. YAMANE WAS sitting in a chair in the staff-room. He wore brand-name eyeglasses. He had once quit smoking but had apparently started up again, and was dragging on a cigarette with a look of satisfaction. He had gotten older. His expression was cheerful, but his face was weather-beaten, and though his hair had always been white in my memory, his shoulders were now noticeably thinner.

"You look good. Thank you for coming. How is your job going?" he said.

Grasping both of his outstretched hands, I replied, "It's fine." The corners of his eyes crinkled in a smile, and his white teeth were beautiful. I couldn't bear to look him in the face.

With a gesture, he sent the woman who had accompanied me from the room and got right down to business. "What is this favor you want to ask?"

Despite his kindness in being the one to broach a difficult topic, I had fallen speechless.

"Don't worry. You don't need to hold back. When I say I'm like a father to you children, those aren't mere

words. I always had a fond impression of you in particular as a child. Whatever it is, you can tell me."

"That . . ."

"What is it?"

"I need . . . money. Would . . . would you be my
guarantor? I promise not to cause any trouble, that . . ."

I still couldn't look him in the face, but I told
myself I was being cowardly, so I forced myself to
raise my gaze. His brows were knit in a frown. Then,
as if trying to recall something, he looked at me with
anxious eyes.

"I see . . . so what will you use it for?"

"I need it for something. And right away. I promise,
I won't cause you any trouble."

No matter what I said, it sounded like an excuse.
That's just the nature of favors involving money.

"How much?"

". . . About three hundred thousand."

"Do you have any other debts?"

"None."

"I might as well lend you that amount myself. If you
borrow it from a broker, they'll charge you interest,
won't they?"

"No, that's too much. Just being my guarantor is more than enough."

Mr. Yamane laughed when I said this. "I get it. It's fine. Don't look so upset. When you made that face, it reminded me of your father. But remember this. You mustn't borrow any more money. Got it?"

"Yes. I promise."

There were a number of pictures drawn by the children posted on the wall. Some were vivid, their subjects easy to identify, but others were just dyed smudges of black and brown. Mr. Yamane got up from his seat, turning his back to me as he looked out the window. The boy was still crossing and uncrossing his arms. I wondered if Mr. Yamane was watching him.

"Have your nightmares gone away?"

"Yes."

"And the feeling of pressure on your chest?"

". . . It's gone."

"Really? That's good."

He waved to someone outside. I figured he might be responding to the boy on the jungle gym.

"When you first came here, your illness was quite serious. You must remember?"

"Yes."

"It was more psychological than physical. That asshole of a doctor said he had rarely seen anything like it, that your recovery would be difficult."

I felt a jolt in my heart, as if it had been stabbed, and then suffocated by an oppressiveness that seemed to originate from within me. The serious illness that he referred to—I had thought it was purely physical.

*"This is the first time I've seen such severe symptoms induced by fear.* That's what the asshole said. I got angry because he acted as if psychiatrists could explain everything with their theories."

Mr. Yamane was looking at my face as if he had seen something there for the first time. Sweat trickled behind my ears, and I felt thirsty. My breathing was labored, and the drops of liquid that ran down my neck were surprisingly cool. My body suddenly felt chilled. My hearing was unusually acute. It was as if his low voice, like a murmur, was reverberating directly in my brain.

"That quack said, '*He suffered prolonged emotional trauma from fear—like a habit, the fear has become part* of his flesh and blood, so it is now second nature to him. Presently, he is seeking out fear. Rather than becoming a part of him, fear has eroded his body, and he is held captive by it—he is dependent upon it. The extent of this self-drive toward fear creates an illness that is eating him away . . .' I remember thinking, I'll be damned, that's just not possible. I asked around later and found out that doctor might have been a medical resident. Just because these kids are in an orphanage, people seem to think they can treat them like damned guinea pigs. In other words . . ."

He looked at me, both his eyes wider than I'd ever seen them.

"In other words, that's the kind of person you are."

Without moving his wild-eyed gaze from mine, he opened his mouth, his lips hanging in a warped expression. I swallowed, unable to take my eyes off his face.

"That's the kind of person you are."

"What—?"

"You are garbage. You're like a piece of trash. You know it, don't you? In this world, there are those who are lucky as shit and those who are shit out of luck.

Nothing you can do about it. You are like the slag that's left behind—you are the excrement of this world.

"You're a freak who takes pleasure from fear. You'd be better off dead. Those like you, their place is to die. You ought to have died back then, when you were in the earth. The person who's here now is just a husk left over after what happened back then. If there's a God, then in God's eyes, you are outside of the plan, an error in calculation."

Intertwined with the words in my ears, a pain thrummed in my head, gradually taking on a rhythm as it formed a writhing mass. Everything around me was dim. All of the faces in the pictures on the wall were smiling as they looked down upon me.

"Get it? We don't need people like you. Isn't that right? You freak—you're better off dead. There's no use wasting my thoughts on such a disgusting, twisted person. I wish you had just died. The meaning of your life was merely to elicit sympathy for your death."

"You're wrong—plenty of people who have been through experiences like this grow up to be normal, stable adults."

"Do you really think so? Of course, you're probably

right. But right now, I'm talking about you. Not anyone else. This is about *you*. You're a monstrosity. For God's sake, hurry up and die."

"Shut up!"

"For God's sake, just do it!"

"Shut the fuck up!"

The chair fell over, and as the sound of breaking glass echoed, I found myself standing up. This middle-aged man was standing before me, baring his white teeth. "Calm down!" he shouted, gripping both of my shoulders and shaking me violently. I couldn't speak, I gasped for breath—I couldn't seem to get any air. He caught me with both arms and tried to squeeze even harder. His skin was on my skin.

*"You're not me!" I shout, and I try to escape but I cannot move. The others are clinging to me. They are clinging to me, trying to get inside of me. I am trembling with fear, and I feel a revulsion—as if it's about to seep from within my skin—it becomes an intense shiver that erodes my body. "You're not me!" I shout, as if gasping for air. "You're not me!"*

My vision went dim as I struggled. Suddenly, Mr. Yamane was embracing me. The woman who had greeted me at the door was there, too, and she drew closer; through the window, children were peering inside. We were in the staff room. Mr. Yamane was shouting, "What just happened?" *Was he talking to me?* He was looking straight at me, so he must have been, right? He was shouting at me to calm down, and asking me what was wrong. I heard various voices. They were calling out to me. Right—I needed to calm down. I had to do as they said and calm down.

THE DYING FLUORESCENT bulb flickered in an irregular rhythm. Mr. Yamane was standing over me, looking down with concern. Apparently I had been put to bed. Our eyes met, but I had no idea what to say.

"Does that kind of thing happen to you often?"

He was looking at me sadly through narrowed eyes. I had seen this expression many times before.

"No."

"But what happened wasn't normal. What's the matter?"

"That . . . I was exhausted. I've been working too much overtime."

"... Really?"

His look of sympathy did not change. The more sincere his expression, the less able I was to tolerate it. I had to say something, it didn't matter what.

"What is Toku doing now?"

"Hmm?"

"Toku. He was here at the same time I was ..."

"... I remember. I'll never forget. He's dead."

"What?"

"He ... killed himself. It happened right after he turned twenty ... It seems he ... he couldn't shed the traumas of his past." He lit a cigarette, as if to distract himself. "For that to happen to someone like him ... I simply can't bear to think about it. You understand, don't you?"

I nodded, but there was nothing else for me to say.

9

Beyond the sound of the shovel digging up the earth and the beam of a flashlight feebly illuminating the darkness, I had a hazy vision of their expressions as they spoke hurriedly to each other, their faces twitching as if they were frightened. I lay there, looking up at them as, shovelful by shovelful, the earth was heaved on top of my small body. I recognized the scene before my eyes for what it was—the culmination of their unrelenting violence toward me. I had only just woken up, but I was overcome by extreme drowsiness. Except this sleepiness was clearly different from normal; it felt as if I were being coerced, like it was impossible to resist. The sounds and voices faded away while my body was gradually pushed down further. My mouth filled with earth and sand. Yet I couldn't muster the energy or the desire to spit it out. It was all I could do to suppress a weak urge to cough.

I opened my eyes one more time, and I was inside the earth. My clothes were wet from the moisture in the soil, and they felt pleasantly cool. I drifted off to sleep again, yearning for the time in my mother's womb, which surely had been just like this. Through my grogginess, I was aware that my skin was enmeshed in particles of dirt. The earth was eroding me, and I would erode the earth. How I wished I could become one with the earth and disappear. There was no need for me to do anything. I didn't need to wait with bated breath to see what their mood was, I didn't need to run about trying to evade their raised fists, I didn't need to protect my head and belly. The earth softly soothed me, cooling me little by little, the chill penetrating deeper into me. There was no hunger or fear here. The earth sequestered me from the rest of the world, completely and securely, and I could die, just like this. I put my thumb in my mouth to reassure myself. My body was growing cold. The drowsiness was different from before, absolute yet gentle, slowly swaying my brain. *This is how it ends*, I thought. When all was said and done, the world had let me go gently.

But something clamored within me. With my attention drawn to this stirring, it grew louder and louder. I wondered what it could be. I thought about how I might describe it, to put it into words. After a moment, the question that came to mind was, *Are you really convinced?* But convinced of what, I wasn't sure. This thought grew louder, as if it had a will of its own. Wasn't there something strange about all this? Was I really okay with it? Didn't I still need to consider the question of why I had these feelings of doubt, and to do so from above ground? When I moved my arms weakly, my breathing became forced, as if I had awakened from something. My body grew heavy. It felt as though the heaviness was pushing down on me, crushing me. I gasped, all the blood in my body seemingly rushing to my head. *I am definitely not convinced of this.* The muscles all over my body began to convulse, quivering incessantly. *This is strange. Something is wrong.* With all my effort, I tried to bend at the abdomen to raise my torso. But, held back by the weight of the earth shrouding my body, I couldn't get up no matter how much I struggled. I moved my arms, trying to dig my way to the surface, but the earth cascaded down on me anew. Drowning, I gagged and sputtered out the earth that I kept swallowing. I could no longer tell up from down. Sensing a solid layer of earth against my knees, flailing my hands about, I thrust at the earth with my head as if to kick my center of gravity into place. The rough particles of dirt were scraping away the surface of my face. After one last vigorous heave, the earth that had covered me was driven upward, and then fluttered back down to settle on top of my head, which had broken through and was now above ground. Still sputtering earth, I let the sudden rush of hot air flood into my lungs. From the chest up, I emerged from the ground and looked around. The peculiar absence of light was so complete, the darkness so overwhelming, that I thought to myself, *I must be somewhere in the mountains.*

No matter how hard or how far I stared into the dark, I could not find a single point of light. With my eyes gradually adjusting to the pitch-black, I could make out the depths of the shadows that formed tall, thin trees with leaves growing only high up on their trunks. My chilled body thawed in the outside air, and my damp clothing dried out slowly. Lying prostrate on the ground, I drank some water from a nearby puddle; it tasted gritty but it seemed to revive me. My awareness began to come around, and I felt a faint stirring in my arms and legs. *I have to get out of here*, I thought. I didn't know what I would do once I left, but I wanted to flee as quickly as I could from the utter nighttime silence enveloped by these infinite trees.

Yet no matter how far I walked, there was no change in my surroundings. The trees stood indifferent to my presence; sometimes there would be a slight incline or slope, the ground was covered everywhere with dirt and fallen leaves. The almost total lack of variation gave me the creeps, as if I were walking around in circles, and bit by bit I started to freak out. All around me were cold, vast rows of trees—a series of straight lines extending to the sky, enclosing me, confining me within their bounds, deliberate and calculating. My legs ached, and sweat poured from all over my body. But once the wind blew, my surroundings were completely transformed. Within the howling that seemed to cut through the air, all of the trees began to sway. In the darkness, those writhing clusters of leaves seemed to press upon me like a single enormous living thing, and I had the impression they were coming after me as they raised a thunderous roar that sounded like a shriek. I cowered in fear—there was no way I could keep walking. I picked up a thick branch that had fallen off a tree and clutched it with all my might. Regardless of my fear, I had to keep walking in the same direction, I told myself. Even if it were the wrong direction, I had no other choice.

I saw a shadow move before me, and I couldn't breathe—my entire body convulsed with fright. There were two creatures, about as tall as my chest, that were slowly, slowly moving toward me. They were stray dogs. These were distinctly different from house dogs; they were fat, their howling yelps murky, their ragged and damp breathing asserting their hunger and clearly signaling that whatever action I might take would have no effect. I was filled with despair. It seemed as if my whole body was plunging further and further, ceaselessly. The fact that I didn't have any food with me could only mean that I was their target. That must be the case, I thought. After all that, this was to be my fate; I had managed to break free from that confined room and that earthen tomb only to be met with obstacles at every turn. I no longer had the strength to run. Slowly, the dogs closed the distance between us.

But right at that moment, I felt a great emotion stir within me like a furious maelstrom. This burgeoning swell seemed to seize control, overwhelming my frightened self and taking over, so that before I knew it, I had let forth a piercing cry, wrenched from my guts. This despite the fact that I thought my voice was gone. At that moment, my cry was not directed toward the dogs. It was directed beyond them, beyond even the people who had tormented me, toward the unseen fate that I was sure existed, deep within the darkness, the fate that brutally manipulated people and living things—I was railing against all existence. *I am alive! Against all of your expectations! I*

*have no intention of obeying you. With my own hands, I*
*will defeat whatever obstacles you throw at me.*.

Clutching with both hands the wooden bough I
had been holding, I sprang toward the dogs. With all
my strength, I let out a keening shriek as I brought the
branch down without knowing where it would land. A
dull vibration ran through both my arms, and enduring
the numbing desire to let go, I waved and swung the
tree limb, striking out again and then again. The instant
I heard a growl behind me, I turned around and raised
the branch. I held my arms overhead and tried to
make myself appear as large as I could. I knew I had
to move faster than my opponents. There was no time
for hesitation. My blow missed its mark, but the dog
turned its back and ran away. I let out another cry and,
adrenaline rushing through me, I swung the bough
and made as if to chase after it. As I watched the dog
flee, the strength drained from my entire body and
I nearly crumpled on the spot. I made myself keep
walking. There was still no change to the surrounding
landscape. The vast rows of trees were all the more
indifferent as they maintained their silence.

After that I don't know how far I walked. I crossed

over countless slopes, drank from countless puddles, passed amongst countless trees. My surroundings gradually turned blue, and when they became illuminated by a faint glow, I realized how long it had been since I had seen the light of day. I was in a daze, and as I felt myself awash in the sunlight, I collapsed where I was. The rays were warm and gentle, and they did their best to infuse the slightly chilled air with heat. When I closed my eyes, I saw pale blue behind my eyelids and I smelled the warm scent of earth. My memory broke off at that point.

IN THE END, I was found by a middle-aged couple who were out for a walk, and they brought me to a hospital. There was a hiking trail on the mountain where I had been buried, and without realizing it, I had made my way to one of the branches of the trail before lying down.

When I awoke in the hospital bed, the doctors had all sorts of questions for me. In those dim and empty surroundings, left with only myself to rely on, I calmly conveyed the facts as I remembered them, one by one. "They" showed up while I was sleeping and made certain threats, but this was after I had told the doctors everything. The man made a fist, and his face was ugly as he muttered at me. Later the detectives arrived and arrested them, and there was an article in the newspaper.

MR. YAMANE TOOK me in a car that went up the small hill toward the orphanage. That road seemed incredibly long—it truly felt as if it would never end. During the ride, Mr. Yamane's shoulders were slumped, and he looked like he was holding back his anger. Although he didn't say a word, it seemed he was terribly disappointed in my real parents' indifference once the authorities had located them and told them what had happened to me. Mr. Yamane was emphatic as he explained to me how to get past this. "Grow up big and strong. If you do that, then you'll be able to live your own life, for yourself."

For me, whose life had always been empty, it wasn't until about a month had passed that I understood my new surroundings. I started school, and while sitting out in gym class, I would suddenly feel as if I had awakened from a light sleep. "Is this what he meant by living my own life?" I remember wondering, as my brain sorted out the same eerie parade of images, one after another. The smiling faces of my classmates throwing a ball back and forth, and the amused voice of the teacher as he called out directions. Me, sitting beside the blue podium for the morning assembly with my knees pulled up to my chest. These images flitted through the back of my mind; the days after I left the hospital were like a fog. Was this my reward? I had dug myself out of the violence, I had crawled from inside the earth, I had come down from the mountain—was this day-to-day routine all I got for it? I didn't under-stand why they were smiling and laughing. Was there something I was missing? I wondered if there was joy in this world equivalent to the level of violence I knew—like the sheer joy I felt when I'd survived, when my entire body would not stop trembling—did anything like that exist here?

I grew even more introverted than I had been before, and I started reading books. As I read the sto-ries written by those who had come before me, I tried to discover just what this world was about, and what was symbolized in these depictions of life.


ONCE THERE WAS a fire at the orphanage, and the novels that I had been collecting over the years were burned. A student who lived nearby had failed his university entrance exams and he was the one who set the fire. The old wooden orphanage must have looked like it would easily catch flame, and the sight of us running this way and that trying to escape probably made him feel superior. After the fire, I wept. You can buy new books, Mr. Yamane said, but I found it difficult to restrain my tears.

**10**

I drove my tenth customer of the night to a business hotel, then got out of the car and lit a cigarette. The last train on the Yurakucho line would be leaving soon, so if I hung around downtown, I could still pick up another fare. It might have been because I had changed to a twenty-one-hour split shift, but I was feeling better. Today's take was already more than fifty thousand.

I switched off the taxi radio and, in the stillness

that enveloped the buildings, stared up at the moon-
less night sky. The confusion that I had felt at the
orphanage unexpectedly flitted through my mind, but
I tried my best not to think about it. Anyhow, I needed
to allow the flow of daily life to carry me along. That
meant going to work, paying back the loan in a timely
manner and, one by one, fulfilling the responsibilities
that came from living a life. My only endeavor was
to bury myself in just that kind of everyday routine.
A call came in on the radio dispatch, but the pickup
location was miles away. Work was work, but there
was still some luck involved.

As I was writing in my fare log, a couple of young
guys approached the cab and gave the name of a hotel
as their destination. I wasn't familiar with the hotel,
but they said it was along the Arakawa River, so after
they got in I hit the gas without even looking at a map.
I asked them for more details about the location and
realized it wasn't far away at all. If I hurried back, I
could probably still get a good spot in the line of taxis
waiting by the bars. I had turned the radio back on for
the customers, and today's news was on. A little girl
had been killed by her mother. The mother had held

the child underwater in the bath until she stopped moving. The announcer read the mother's statement as if it were nothing. No matter what kinds of tragedies occurred, the world kept spinning—perhaps it was the natural order of things. The news ended, a pop song came on, and there was a plug for the latest movie. *Amongst the laughter, a dispassionate sorrow glimmers*, a guest commentator intoned about the film.

And then there was a knife pointed at my neck. "Shut up and drive." As the low voice echoed in my ear, my entire body went rigid, and a strained vigor rose in my throat, suffocating me. His voice a drawl, the second guy mumbled something in a language I didn't recognize—not Japanese or English. The guy with the knife tried to grab my bag by the driver's seat.

My arms tensed as they gripped the steering wheel. I hadn't realized it until now, but my taxi was the only car on the road. It took me a while to grasp the situation. *Was this a taxi robbery?* The moment the thought occurred to me, the words almost escaped my lips, but somehow I managed to suppress them. The money I had worked for all day long was about to be stolen from me. I felt a shooting pain in my neck, and then what I assumed were warm drops of blood. My heart was pounding, and because I was driving, my gaze was straight ahead, but the scenery didn't register. I no longer even knew where we were. The knife at my throat barely touched my skin, then it moved away, and then I felt it again. The guy speaking a foreign language was saying something. As I tried to settle my ragged breathing, I repeated to myself, *Get it together*, over and over in my mind. Should I slam on the brakes, grab back the bag, and get the hell out of the car? Or should I just stay calm and accept that the money was gone? These conflicting ideas collided bewilderingly as fear maintained its steady grip on me, until I didn't think I'd be capable of carrying out whichever course of action I decided to take.

"That's right, don't get any ideas. Just keep driving."

The second man spoke to him in whatever the foreign language was.

"What? No, we don't have to go that far, do we?"

The guy I couldn't understand was shouting something. The guy holding the knife was trying to calm him down, but that only seemed to make him more insistent.

"No, with this much money, we don't need to bother with that," and then something unintelligible.

They went back and forth; I couldn't comprehend what they were saying to each other. As if an indeterminate anxiety were seeping through my body, my focus blurred and the strength drained unpleasantly from my arms, making it difficult to drive. They were still arguing, and when I checked to see them in the rearview mirror, the guy speaking a foreign language was violently bashing the seat, over and over and over again. The guy holding the knife was trying to persuade him. But the guy speaking a foreign language refused to be convinced.

I felt thirsty, but a prodigious amount of sweat poured from all over my body. At the very least, my attempt to figure out what they were saying helped to focus my attention on listening. I still had no idea what language they were speaking.

Their argument ended, and a tense stillness descended inside the car. Despite the fact that I was the one driving, I had the impression that the taxi was taking me somewhere of its own accord. There were no cars anywhere nearby. No cars, and not even a single shop's light could be seen.

". . . Come on, you don't have to be so scared," the guy holding the knife muttered in my ear.

His expression was distinctly different from before. His eyes were bloodshot, his face pale, his breathing rough—it seemed like he had decided on something and was worked up about it. The guy speaking the foreign language had curled his lower lip into a strange angle. From where I sat, it appeared to be a smirk of satisfaction.

"Let's do it here, stop here."

We were at a construction site surrounded by tall buildings. An excavator had been left sitting there, along with various iron and steel materials and a pile of excavated sand, with the steel framework of the building towering above, seemingly floating in midair. I was pulled by the hair, the knife still held to my throat as we got out of the taxi. The breeze carried a chill that instantly cooled my perspiration. There were several streaks of blood trickling down my neck. I was pushed down onto the mound of sand.

"Sorry . . . It wasn't the plan, but . . . now you have to die."

I was helpless as the man who had been holding the knife strangled me. His fat fingers tightened around my throat. I pushed back against him with both hands, trying to escape, but I had no strength. I gasped for breath, feeling the bile rise in my throat, but I couldn't even manage to throw up. I grabbed the guy's sleeve, but there was nothing else I could do. I didn't have the strength for it. Blood rushed to my face and my skin felt like it would burst. My eyes watered. They felt as if they were about to pop out of my head as I struggled, and the hideous face of the guy before me, a half-smile on his lips, went blurry. *Not in a place like this*, I thought, and at that moment, my field of vision went white and, incredibly, the pain gradually eased. *Sleep*, I thought. *No!* This isn't sleep! This isn't sleep . . . My young self was there before me. Or rather, this was the me here now. I was clinging to the balcony railing. Before now, I had never had any memory of this. But there it was, having appeared within my mind as if it were right in front of me, as clear as day. The man's massive arms held my sides and tried to hoist me up. There was no strength left in my right hand, which was clutching the railing and, irrespective of my will, my grip released as simply as that. The man was drunk. "It's only the second floor, so you won't die," he sang in a loud voice. "It's only the second floor, so you won't die," he sang as he held my frail body high in the air. My body cowered in terror and tears sprang to my eyes, but at that moment an emotion stirred within me—a single determination welled up like a mass of energy. "Enough!" The word flashed in my head. I didn't need to keep enduring this. There was no need to be afraid. He might really intend to hurl me by the force of his arms. And if I fell from this height I might actually die. But I tried to accept the fear. This fear was like my own flesh and blood . . . and it was at that moment when I felt as though I had surpassed them—me, in my wretched squalor. *I do not fear your violence. It has no effect on me.* Not all the violence in the world—no matter how wanton or unreasonable—I refused to be afraid of it. I tried to smile. There was no need for me to surrender. I would die smiling. Maybe I could use this—so that even if I died, I still won. My body rose in the air, and I started to fall. The ground—and my own death—was speeding toward me. I could hear the man's laughter ring out like a shriek. But I was the one who would conquer. I would not surrender—not to any of the foolish people in this world, not to any of the violence or atrocity . . .

When I came to, I was lying on my back in the earth. Amid the sound of the shovel digging up the earth and the beam of a flashlight feebly illuminating the darkness, I coughed. Or I tried to. The guy who had been holding the knife was on top of me, looking down at me with wide, wild eyes. I tried to cough a few more times, and each time, it felt as though I couldn't get enough air into my lungs. The guy let out a yell and reached for my throat again. I was in agony. But despite the intense pain around my neck, I became aware of something stiff in my pocket. It was the ballpoint pen I had been using to write in my fare log. Somehow I got it out and thrust it into the guy's thigh. He screamed and slumped over, away from me. Still coughing, I ran toward the taxi. The guy speaking a foreign language came running after me, shouting something. He grabbed my shoulder, and I spun around and tried to punch him in the face. My fist missed him, but he stumbled, his movements sluggish. I opened the car door, got in, and started the engine. I stepped on the gas. I put all my energy into the foot that was on the gas pedal. I turned the steering wheel onto the road. They were far away from me. I just kept on going straight, the only car on the deserted night streets.

I burst into tears as I drove away. The tears were partly from relief, partly from sadness—I didn't really know. I thought about the fact that I was still alive and, as I gripped the steering wheel, I exhaled deeply in an effort to control my breathing. As I recalled an image I had caught a glimpse of, I thought to myself, What if that medical resident had been wrong? What if victory, not fear, was the thing that I wished for? There was a way to conquer the fear that had taken root within me—a way that others might find perplexing—but perhaps I had created the fear just so that I could overcome it, as my own form of resistance to my fate? The road stretched out before me, the light from the evenly spaced streetlamps uninterrupted and unending. Yet I couldn't shake the feeling that, inside me, something wasn't quite right.

It was trivial, but the more I tried to put it out of my mind, the more it became a twinge in my stagnant consciousness, the more it clamored within me. My right foot was heavy on the gas, as if compelled by that twinge. *Could I really know for sure?* I murmured the words as the needle on the speedometer slanted to the right, as if it were being spurred in that direction. *I feel kind of strange*, I thought, and right at that moment it was as if my body were falling at an accelerated speed. My heart experienced a heavy shock, as if I had been struck. There was a sharp curve in front of me. As if I could see the scene in miniature, it seemed to be heading toward me with tremendous speed. *That is the ground*, I thought. Everything sped up. I kept going faster, and I kept falling. The white of the guardrail was right before me. It expanded, as if it were going to attack me, trying to crush me. My heart throbbed with palpitations, and I could not move, as if my muscles were frozen. It felt as if the only thing left inside my body was a single mass, and it was falling. I had left my fear behind me. When I saw the guardrail close at hand, its white color seemed to glimmer warmly and gently at me. As the crush of the impact ripped through my body and the various noises swelled, crashed, then subsided, I felt as if I were filling up with something soft and cool.

11

A white light floated in the air, growing hazy with mist. The more I tried to focus on the whiteness, the less distinct its contours became and the more I was left with just the afterimage of an indeterminate brilliance. I opened my mouth to speak. There was a brief lapse in time before I felt certain that the hoarse sound breaking from my throat was my own voice.

My neck was fixed in place, though I was able to

move everything else. But when I tried to raise my right arm, a stabbing pain concentrated at the base of my throat, and it became a struggle to breathe. The afterimage that remained behind my eyes had faded to green, and it swayed from side to side whenever my gaze shifted. My conversation with the doctor drifted through my mind. I had a feeling that I had tried to make all kinds of excuses. Yesterday's events were similarly obscure. The quilt had been pulled up to my shoulders, but I had a slight chill, and it seemed unlikely I would fall back asleep.

The door opened and Sayuko came in. Seeing her on crutches, my memories of recent events came flooding back. "You're finally awake," she said, giving me a smile. Unable to make much effort, I let out a little sound in acquiescence.

"The two of us are really giving this hospital a lot of business," she joked, as if she didn't know what else to say, and smiled again. She opened a folding chair with one hand and sat down, stretching out her bandaged leg.

". . . How are you feeling?" Her expression was somewhat drawn.

"Not great. Even if I could move my neck, I can't get out of bed."

"After an accident like that, it's a miracle you're not in worse shape." She raised her downcast gaze, slowly and hesitantly. When she did, her eyes were tinged with the shadow of reproach. ". . . It's a lie, isn't it? You said you were out of your head when you crashed, from your escape after being robbed . . . But even if you were really robbed, the rest of it is a lie, isn't it? You crashed on purpose. Why? Why do such a thing?"

Her lips were trembling, but her gaze was stern and unwavering. I closed my eyes, but was unable to stem the emotion centered between my brows.

"I don't know why," I replied frankly. "I just . . . felt like it would be a gentle way to go. You know, like maybe it would be the easiest thing—and then nothing more would happen to me, you know? At that moment, the world seemed gentle. Astonishingly so."

"What the hell are you talking about? How is dying going to help anything?"

"Not dying . . . That's not what I'm talking about— not exactly." My voice trembled with the words.

"When I was about to crash, I felt like I was totally one with myself, and I couldn't stop it."

"That's stupid." She started to cry. "You said you'd always be there for me, didn't you? Were you lying? This is cruel. You're such a—such a coward!"

"You're right. I'm sorry."

The moonlight streaming through the window had cast a shadow on Sayuko's teary face. I could hear a child making noise in the room next to us. The moon was beautiful, and the echo of the child's clear voice made a lovely sound. The shadow created by the curtain extended out straight, as if to divide the hospital room.

"And . . . The people who did that to you, they aren't around anymore, are they?" she murmured.

". . . I know that."

"No, you don't . . . ! They're gone! The people who attacked you are gone now." Sayuko's words resonated with warmth and kindness. Yet something inside me still resisted. I wondered, *Could that really be true . . . ?* The child's voice quieted, and I could now hear the faint sound of the television from the next room. The announcer was reading the latest news in a businesslike manner.

"For some reason, I feel like crying," I said, and she laughed.

"It's all right if you cry, isn't it? I'm the only one here."

AT THE EAST exit of Ikebukuro Station, in front of where the Seibu Ikebukuro Line let out, there was a constant stream of people, despite it being a weekday. All of them jumbled together, noisily rushing about in every direction in the darkening bluish gloom of evening, the countless neon signs advertising themselves but still only dimly illuminating their surroundings. In the past, being in a crowd like this would have made me feel isolated and alone; I would have hated it. The people gathered together had seemed like an amorphous haze bearing down on me—I'd felt a sense of oppression. I probably still felt it, but I wasn't quite as aware of it now. I had only just gotten out of the hospital, but as long as I took it easy, I could walk without pain in my neck. I lit a cigarette and looked for Mr. Yamane, whom I was meeting here.

Despite her own injury, Sayuko had done a lot for

me while I was laid up. On crutches, she went to the hospital shop, and when they didn't have what I needed, she refused to be deterred—no matter what I said—and got herself to a convenience store. The nurse told me over and over about the way she made it down the staircase, swinging her thin body from step to step. I didn't see it for myself, but I could easily imagine it. From now on, I would have to measure up to her.

I spotted Mr. Yamane beside the pedestrian crossing. He raised his hand in my direction.

"I'm sorry, I thought I was right on time—am I late?"

"No, uh, I got here too early. You're fine."

For some reason, Mr. Yamane didn't seem entirely relaxed. *We should get dinner sometime,* he had said, but I had the feeling there was something specific he wanted to say to me. He was chain-smoking, more so than usual, and smiling constantly. This time, I figured it would be my turn to listen.

"Is there something you're afraid to say? It's all right—just tell me."

"Ah, uh-hmm, actually, I feel terrible about this."

He stubbed out his cigarette and lit a new one. "The restaurant where I planned for us to go tonight— your father is supposed to be there. If I had told you beforehand, I figured you probably wouldn't come . . . Ah, of course, I have no particular wish to bring you two together, but . . . he insisted, you see. He probably has a favor or something he wants to ask of you. 'Let me see him myself,' he said, since I wouldn't give him your contact information. He even told me I had no right to refuse him. He's probably right. But I arranged this meeting on the condition that I be here as well."

With an apologetic look, Mr. Yamane spoke slowly, choosing his words as he gauged my response. I hated to think about causing such a good man to worry. I smiled to reassure him that it was all right.

"Do you remember the 'Mercy Event'? About six months after I came to the orphanage."

"Hm?"

"The 'Mercy Event.' Right after I came to the orphanage."

Mr. Yamane looked at me blankly, but then nodded.

"There were tons of donations. Most of it was

clothing. But these weren't just the usual hand-me-down donations—surprisingly everything was brand-new. The local businesses that had collected the donations were very kind, and we all sang a song in gratitude."

A car sped up to go through the pedestrian crossing, where the light had changed and the sound was signaling for us to cross. In front of us, a little girl spun around in surprise. Mr. Yamane had stopped inhaling his cigarette and was looking me in the face.

"But I wasn't the least bit happy about it. I hated being made to wear the clothes, even that they had been given to me, and when the adults asked me what was wrong, I refused to answer. I just sulked in silence . . . Some of the other children became infected with my antipathy, and it almost ruined the event. The employees from the businesses had made the effort to bring these things to us, and I had disgraced everyone. I had repaid their goodwill with hostility, and my behavior caused distress for many people. And the orphanage had been indebted to these businesses for a long time . . . "

Mr. Yamane had closed his eyes. His face was calm;

the deep creases that appeared on his visage reminded me, once again, how old he was now.

"When the event ended, and we all started to clean up . . . I thought I was going to be beaten. I had made those employees feel ashamed, and my attitude must have caused trouble for everyone, so I thought I would be severely reprimanded. When you came over to me, my entire body was bracing for a beating. I knew if I prepped myself, I could stand it, at least to a certain extent. But Mr. Yamane, you didn't beat me. On the contrary, you smiled and patted me on the cheek. I could not make sense of it. I couldn't understand why you didn't hit me. I just stood there, still holding a chair that I had been about to put away, unable to move. I'll never forget that moment. If nothing else, no matter what happens, I will always remember that moment. Up until now, I have not been focused on what is important. I'm not talking about just back then. Mr. Yamane, you are still to this day looking out for me . . . I am truly grateful to you."

I bowed my head as I spoke these words, and made as if to turn around to go back the way we had come.

"Hey." Mr. Yamane's voice was loud and frantic. "Of course I can understand if you don't want to see him, but don't you think you should meet him, just this once? You would have had a different life if he hadn't left you in the first place, right? Don't you have anything to say to him? After all you've been through?"

I turned back around to face Mr. Yamane again.

"I was born in the earth."

"What?"

"I have no parents. Not any more. They mean nothing to me now."

I turned my back and started walking into the crowd waiting for me, so thick that I couldn't see in front of me. The hordes of people passed by me, as crowds do, every imaginable expression visible on various faces, each person walking in their own direction. I thought I might have seen "them" among the throng, which gave me a little start, but I kept my eyes open and walked on past. Mr. Yamane did not call out after me, but I assumed he was still back there, watching me. I stepped slowly through the chaos. No matter which way I headed, there was an endless flow of people.

I was planning to take Sayuko on a little trip, once I was a bit more settled back into my life. But first, before we decided on anything or made any demands, I thought we should pay a visit to her child's grave.

# Afterword

*The Boy in the Earth* was the fifth book I wrote.

I have truly been saved by literature. If I hadn't met with stories that dive deep into the nature of society and humanity, stories that press on and attempt to reveal our true nature, I'm sure my life would have turned out differently. Literature is still precious to me. It provides me with the sustenance I need to go on living. Even now, having come to write books myself, that hasn't changed in the slightest.

I want to thank everyone who helped me publish this book, and all the people who will read it.

—Fuminori Nakamura

# About the Author

Fuminori Nakamura was born in 1977 and graduated from Fukishima University in 2000. He has won numerous prizes for his writing, including the Ōe Prize, Japan's largest literary award; the David L. Goodis Award for Noir Fiction; the Shinchō and Nōma Prizes for debut fiction; and the Akutagawa Prize, Japan's most prestigious literary award. *The Thief*, his first novel to be translated into English, was a finalist for the *Los Angeles Times* Book Prize, was selected by *The Wall Street Journal* as best fiction of the year, and a World Literature Today Notable Translation. His works have been translated into numerous languages and made into several films. His other novels that have been published in English include *The Gun*, *Evil and the Mask*, *The Kingdom*, and *Last Winter, We Parted*.

# About the Translator

Allison Markin Powell is a literary translator and editor in New York City. Her translation of *The Briefcase* by Hiromi Kawakami was nominated for the 2012 Man Asian Literary Prize, and the UK edition (*Strange Weather in Tokyo*) was nominated for the 2014 Independent Foreign Fiction Prize. She has also translated works by Osamu Dazai and Kanako Nishi, among others.

*Continue reading for a preview of*

# CULT X

"She's alive."

The bar's blue lights faintly illuminated Naraza-ki's face. Their malicious glow seemed to bleach the color from his body. *Has his face always looked like that?* Kobayashi wondered. He looked like he'd lost something he needed to go on living. Yet his gaze was terribly powerful, and had a strange radiance.

"She's really alive?" Narazaki's voice was rough.

"I wouldn't lie, and it's no mistake. Ryoko Tachibana is alive." The woman who had vanished from Narazaki's life, who had hinted at suicide and then disappeared.

Kobayashi realized quite a bit of his whiskey was gone. His hand was moving his glass to his lips automatically. He was almost unsure he was in control of it.

"Okay, look." Kobayashi hesitated. "I don't think you should get involved."

"Why?"

"Well . . ."

To Kobayashi, Narazaki's relationship with Ryoko Tachibana had always seemed a bit off. When Kobayashi had happened to see her last month, he hadn't had the courage to speak to her, but—maybe it was because of the work he did—he'd decided to tail her. She'd gone into an old apartment building. Without a doubt, it had been her.

"You looked into it for me, right? Tell me what you found."

"Well . . ."

Kobayashi could hear shouting coming from a table at the far side of the room. The voices gradually lost strength and vanished, as if dissolving into the darkness.

A few weeks ago, when Kobayashi had told him he'd seen Ryoko Tachibana, Narazaki had looked surprised, but also seemed to have already known.

Like it somehow made sense to him. Kobayashi had given Narazaki the address of the apartment building, but for some strange reason Narazaki had insisted Kobayashi investigate instead. It was true, Kobayashi did work at a P.I.'s office, but he hadn't even been there six months. So far he'd mostly just assisted the other investigators, and had never worked a case alone. He'd felt a case like this would be too much for him. But he'd taken the job, if reluctantly, and he had actually discovered quite a lot in a short time. There was something odd about that, he thought. *How could someone like me, someone still training, find so much out so easily?*

"Is there some big secret? Something that would hurt me?"

"Not exactly . . ."

A peal of laughter from another distant table. In the dim light of the restaurant, Kobayashi could only make out the outlines of the people laughing. He caught himself drinking again. He was trying to get drunk. Why?

*Should I tell Narazaki what I'm worried about?* Kobayashi wondered. He had all the material he'd collected about Ryoko Tachibana in his bag. She'd been born in Nagasaki Prefecture, had attended elementary through high school there, and then moved to Tokyo to enroll in Rikkyo University. But she'd withdrawn, and that trail of information ended. She next surfaced at a meeting held at the facility of a certain small religious organization in Tokyo—the kind of organization people didn't hear many good things about. But eventually she'd vanished again. She reappeared last year, and that was when she met Narazaki. There were no traces of her life between the time she left that religious organization and when she met him. She'd just somehow appeared before Narazaki, then vanished again.

This religious group also bothered Kobayashi. It was the sort of thing one just shouldn't get involved in.

And now she had already moved out of the apartment he'd seen her enter.

Kobayashi stared listlessly at the counter. The three bartenders looked like triplets. They moved slowly and emotionlessly. Kobayashi shook his head slightly.

"I understand you're puzzled. But, in any case, she's not dead. That I confirmed. And given that . . . Look, what's clear is that she left you. She probably had her reasons. I understand that's not enough to satisfy you, but she left you."

Kobayashi's whole investigation of this woman had felt strange. As he traced her history, it was as if a single line had been prepared for him to follow. Like she was somewhere in the distance, beckoning him. Kobayashi took another sip of whiskey. She should have known he worked at an investigator's office. Had she shown herself to him that first time on purpose? But why? Why would she do that?

"Listen." Kobayashi turned to face Narazaki. "Let me say this clearly. I've got a bad feeling about this. You shouldn't try to find her. There's no need for you to get dragged into whatever this is."

"Why?"

"You have your life."

"My life?"

"You could get hurt."

"That doesn't matter."

Kobayashi would remember, for the rest of his life, Narazaki's next words.

"The life I lived . . . That life has no value at all."

Kobayashi stared for a second at Narazaki's face. In the end, he handed him the envelope filled with everything he'd found about Ryoko Tachibana. There was a small commotion at the table next to them. Kobayashi sipped his whiskey. As he drank, he realized he was getting drunk so he would be able to give the envelope to Narazaki.

He watched Narazaki open the envelope, wondering what his role was. If this were a novel, he probably wouldn't be anything more than a side character. Whatever happened to whom, it would have nothing to do with him. He'd just be the cog that happened to set things in motion.

The other customers gradually headed home. Eventually, only Narazaki and Kobayashi were left in the dim bar. The blue lights illuminated only Narazaki.

Though there was no longer any need for him to drink, Kobayashi ordered another whiskey. His life had no value—that's what Narazaki said. *That may be true*, Kobayashi thought. Even to Kobayashi, Narazaki's life did not seem like a fulfilled one. Certainly, his life was not something anyone would be jealous of. Just like Kobayashi's.

# 1

In front of Narazaki was a gate.

It was an old, enormous wooden gate. There was something written on it, but the characters had faded and Narazaki couldn't make them out. *Should I go straight in?* Narazaki was unsure. *There's something strange about this place. But isn't it just a normal house? It seems more like a house than a church or temple.*

The gate cut through the frigid air and towered over Narazaki. It seemed like it was looking down on him, testing him, about to pass down some sort of judgment. Looking up at the gate, Narazaki was made aware of the smallness of his own body. He wasn't ready to go in, so he walked past. The building was surrounded by tall brick-and-clay walls, and Narazaki couldn't see inside.

He recalled Kobayashi's report. Ryoko Tachibana had certainly belonged to this group. The founder was named Shotaro Matsuo, a man who called himself an amateur intellectual. The group seemed to be some sort of religious organization, but they didn't have a proper name, they weren't registered as a religion, and the whole concept of "believing in" their faith seemed foreign to them. They didn't worship a particular god—in fact, the group's focus seemed to be pondering the question, "Is there a god?"

What were they? Narazaki didn't understand.

As he passed the gate, Narazaki thought to himself, *I always do this. I always hesitate.* It was as though he wanted to spend the rest of his life stuck, the days sinking away heavily. Though they were unhappy, he wanted to savor that unhappiness. The languor seemed to be his very flesh, and he could never leave it. But he had decided to stop living that way. He would follow the pull of the gravity he had begun to feel within himself. He would give himself up to whatever came. He didn't care what would come of it.

He made one loop around the building. *I am walking now*, Narazaki thought. *Walking, without*

*paying attention to anything. How can I walk this way?
Like my heart and other organs just keep moving on
their own. Like they're strangers wriggling in my body.*
Narazaki took a deep breath. *What am I thinking? It's
because of that gate—it's messed up my mind.*

He was here to find out what he could about Ryoko
Tachibana.

He was back in front of the gate. It was still too big.
Just as he was about to open it, he noticed the intercom.
His finger reached toward the button. He wasn't ready.
*What will happen if this is a cult? Maybe they'll lock me
up.* His pulse quickened. *Maybe I'll be brainwashed and
go mad. Maybe I'll wind up one of those paranoid nut jobs
without even realizing I've been brainwashed into acting
that way.* Narazaki pressed the button. He heard a dull
chime. *I pushed it. It's too late now.*

"Yes?" It was the voice of a middle-aged woman.
Not what Narazaki had expected.

"Is Shotaro Matsuo in?"

"To whom am I speaking?"

Narazaki's body tensed up. *No going back now.*

"My name's Toru Narazaki. I'm . . . I'm not really
anyone."

*If I ask where Ryoko Tachibana is right away, they probably won't tell me. I'll just pretend I'm interested in their group, and ask about her a little at a time. I'm not going to join them or anything.* Narazaki realized he was smiling.

"Not anyone?"

"Yeah."

"So you're not with the media?"

"No. If you want, you can look through my things."

"You need to see the old man—I mean, Matsuo-san—about something?"

"Yes."

There was a pause, and then the gate finally opened from the inside. Three people came to meet Narazaki: a middle-aged man and woman and a younger woman. Narazaki had imagined they'd all be dressed in white shrouds or something, but all three were wearing normal clothes. The middle-aged woman had on an apron printed with Rilakkuma, the brown cartoon bear. Narazaki was a bit surprised.

"Please, come in."

Narazaki entered. On the other side of the gate was a large open space. Faintly blue gravel covered the ground, which was scattered with stepping stones. *It looks like a Shinto shrine*, Narazaki thought. But there were no torii gates. There was also a large pond, but there didn't seem to be any koi.

The middle-aged woman in the Rilakkuma apron said, "I'm sorry for asking, but you really aren't with the media?"

"No. I'm just curious about your religion."

"Religion?" asked the middle-aged man. There was a little white in his short-cropped hair, but the expression on his face was youthful. "Well, we don't practice any religion here."

"You don't?"

"It's hard to explain," the younger woman said. "Do you want to learn about healing power?"

"Healing power?" Narazaki asked. He was a bit surprised.

"You're not interested in that? Well then, we should start with his talks."

"Yeah, that's a good idea." The middle-aged man laughed at Narazaki's confusion. "We can let him inside the house, can't we? He doesn't look like he'll cause any harm."

Several people were sitting on the wooden veranda that ringed the mansion. Narazaki felt their stares as he was led from the gate into the house. *Is this okay?* Narazaki wondered. *How are they letting me through so easily?* He had no choice but to follow.

The mansion was large but old, and, compared to the exterior, the inside was unimpressive. Narazaki was taken to a spacious tatami sitting room at least forty square meters in size. Its stillness seemed to be in direct proportion to its size. He took a seat on a cushion.

"Your name was Toru Narazaki, right? I'm Yoshida," said the middle-aged man.

"My name is Mineno, and the woman in the apron is Tanaka-san," the young woman added. Mineno had thin eyes. She was beautiful.

"Where did you hear about us?"

"From a friend."

"A friend? Ah, I see."

What did she see? He had hoped they would press him further. He had answers prepared for them.

The young woman spoke again. "I know you went out of your way to come here, but I'm sorry to say Matsuo-san isn't in."

"He's not here?"

"No. He's been sick."

Yoshida laughed. "It's funny, right? The man heals others, but then goes and gets sick! And on top of that, he can't use his healing powers on himself, so he winds up in a university hospital, getting treated with Western medicine!"

"Shut up!" Mineno told Yoshida. But she was holding back her laughter, too.

What was going on? They were laughing at their leader getting sick?

"We should explain," Mineno said. "Healing power is mostly just a joke. Matsuo-san doesn't really think he can heal people." She smiled. "And it's a bit strange for us to let you in even though he's in the hospital, but we have a rule to not send anyone away."

"How much do you know about this place?" asked Yoshida, as the woman with the Rilakkuma apron came in, carrying tea.

Narazaki thanked her. He still didn't have the courage to say what he wanted. "Honestly, I don't know much."

"That's impressive, showing up without knowing

anything," Yoshida said, laughing. "So, shall we tell you a little about this place? Don't get your hopes up. We're not a religion, so we can't be sure we'll meet your expectations. The people who've shown up lately have come expecting too much. We have to make sure they don't get disappointed and cause any trouble."

HERE WAS WHAT they told him.

Shotaro Matsuo, the owner of the mansion, often meditated alone in his garden.

Long ago, there were no walls, and passers by could see him meditating. He was known in the neighborhood as a weird old man. No one knew about his past, or even if he'd always lived there. It seemed he had just appeared one day in this old mansion that everyone had assumed was abandoned.

One day, an old woman suffering from an inexplicable pain in her legs stopped by. She asked Matsuo to pray over her. Even doctors couldn't figure out what was causing the pain, so she visited every faith healer she could, but she saw no improvement. "You're always sitting here, meditating," she said. "You might have some kind of power. Won't you pray for my legs, just to see?"

Matsuo was surprised, and said he didn't have that sort of power, but he invited the old woman into his mansion for tea. Matsuo lived with his wife, Yoshiko. The three of them talked about many things. Both Matsuo and his wife, Yoshiko, sympathized with the woman's pain. Matsuo tried rubbing the woman's legs, but nothing happened.

"Thank you anyway," the woman said. "Can I come again?"

The Matsuos nodded. She visited for several weeks, and the woman's legs began to get better.

"BUT, LIKE I told you, don't get your hopes up. The cause of that woman's pain was stress," Yoshida said. "That's how religious healers have been treating illnesses forever. Sure, there may be some people who have actual powers, but I can tell you that Matsuo-san isn't one of them. Like Jesus said, faith will save you. That's at least partially true. There are legends that when Jesus Christ first appeared, he cured tons of sick people. It's probably true. If you really believed from the bottom of your heart that this man had the power to cure, that he really was the son of God—well. The human body's ability to cure itself is truly amazing, and stress causes so many ailments. If you're overcome by emotion from seeing God right in front of you, that emotion may activate something amazing inside you."

Yoshida smiled.

"And I think exorcisms are the same sort of thing. Some exorcists may actually drive out evil spirits, but some just *convince* the subject that all the stress inside their body is a single spirit that they can banish. Look, I'm not criticizing anyone for their beliefs. As human civilization has progressed, we've given up on those methods of healing. We no longer recognize gods and spirits as causes of illness, so we don't try to activate the body's own immune system by invoking those things. I'm sure before modern medicine this was an incredibly important form of healing for people."

THE WOMAN WHOSE legs healed spread Matsuo's praise through the town. Gradually, people started

visiting, then claiming their mysterious heart palpitations and their stiff necks got better. Matsuo continued
to tell everyone that he didn't have any special power,
but his insistence began to offend the people who
believed in him. Matsuo truly wanted everyone to
get better, so he found himself in a dilemma. He was
being made a religious figure against his will.

Of course, many people didn't get better. Those
who didn't began to censure Matsuo. It must be awful
to not be healed when others are. Matsuo didn't take
money or anything, so there wasn't too much of a
problem. But little by little this organization began to
change.

"DON'T YOU FEEL calm here?" Mineno asked.

Looking at their smiling faces, Narazaki found it
more and more difficult to breathe.

"There are plenty of trees," Mineno went on, "and
with the gravel garden, all the sound gets sucked up.
It's so peaceful, like being at a shrine."

"That's very true," Narazaki said, his voice emo-
tionless.

"More and more people started saying that just being here makes them feel good. They said maybe instead of healing power, there's just something about being here . . . Maybe this place is what they call a power spot. People have even come from other prefectures. They never seem particularly religious. They're just like, 'We heard there's something here.' Matsuo-san and everyone opened up the garden, and people would say, 'If you got a torii, it would be just like a shrine.' Matsuo-san has always had something about him that attracts people. We started holding an event once a month. We set up a bunch of folding chairs and everyone listens to Matsuo-san speak. It's almost like a natural phenomenon. We've been doing it since the end of the bubble, when society seemed so uneasy."

Narazaki nodded, although he didn't really want to hear more about Matsuo.

Yoshida began speaking again. "Whether you find Matsuo-san's talks interesting or not, they're unique. He never says, 'Believe in this god.' It's more like, 'I wonder if this god's out there.' Even young people like the talks, since he's always questioning. It doesn't cost anything to attend our gatherings, so it's rather low pressure."

Narazaki nodded again. *What should I do?* he thought. *Why is Ryoko Tachibana involved with this kind of group?* He couldn't see why she had to vanish. He had no interest in the history of this group. It was not the religious fringe organization Narazaki had imagined. He'd hoped to stumble into something wilder, something that would change him completely. Something that would make him lose all concern for morals and ethics and the confused human condition. Something that would obliterate him and the life he had lived until now.

Narazaki had no business with these kind people. There was no need to listen to these boring stories. There was no need to hesitate anymore. He spoke up. "There's a woman, Ryoko Tachibana, who I think came here."

They all looked at him.

"What? You're looking for someone? You didn't come to hear about Matsuo-san?"

"Well, that, too. But I'm also looking for this woman."

"We wouldn't know her by that name," Yoshida

said. "There's no membership or registration system here. And people also use fake names."

"This is her," Narazaki said, taking out a photo. Everyone in the room looked at the picture. It was just a few seconds, but it felt infinitely long to Narazaki. The uneasy silence seemed to make the room grow even larger.

"This woman?" Yoshida stared at Narazaki. He was no longer smiling. "How do you know this woman?"

"Wait," Mineno said, as if to stop Yoshida. But she was clearly unsettled. "I'm sorry, but—are you involved with this woman?"

*What happened? They're all looking at me.* Narazaki took a mindful breath. "It's a bit difficult to explain our relationship. But I'm looking for her."

"Why?" Yoshida asked quietly.

*Should I tell them everything? Will I get tangled up in something strange?* Narazaki caught himself smiling. "She ran away."

"Ran away? Do you know what kind of person you're looking for?"

"What kind of person? What do you mean?"

"He doesn't know," Mineno said to Yoshida. "If

he knew about her, he'd know he wouldn't find her here."

"You're right."

The room grew quiet again. The woman in the apron stared at the floor, unsure of what to do.

"Whatever happens, you should probably listen to what we have to say," Mineno said. "It's probably easiest to understand if we explain from the beginning . . . About what happened to Matsuo-san, and the people who came here. I think that will be the easiest way to explain who this woman is . . . And I think you'll want to hear this."

# 2

The wind began to blow gently, causing the windows of the sitting room to rattle as if in pain. *The air is dry*, Narazaki thought. *If I lit a fire, I wonder if it would all burn. The pillars, the ceiling, everything holding this mansion together.*

"Yeah, we should start from the beginning," Mineno said. "It's pretty complicated . . . You were very serious when you showed us this picture. So we should be serious, too, and explain everything thoroughly."

ALL SORTS OF people would gather to hear Matsuo-san speak on the second Saturday of every month. Some people were drawn to his personality, but others saw something sacred in him. Most of those people had been involved with some other religion but had lost hope in their various faiths. There were also suffering youths. People who had been failed by their friends, or lovers, or the companies they worked for, or maybe even another religion. There weren't many, but a few came to study—study how to start their own religion. To use Matsuo's talks as references for their own sermons. Anyone who had been attending the talks for a long time could spot those types immediately. They were always focused on results, and they had voices that cut right through you. They left unpleasant impressions.

There was one man who appeared to be in his fifties who called himself Sawatari, but that may not have been his real name. Five years ago, there was an incident at one of Matsuo's regular Saturday talks. The talks were the most popular they'd ever been. About two hundred people were gathered in the garden. In the middle of speaking, Matsuo suddenly collapsed. Later we learned he'd had a stroke. The moment he fell over, Mineno and the other long-time attendees panicked and rushed to the stage. But from the audience a voice declared that Matsuo had been

possessed by god. I've seen this before, the voice said.
A god has descended upon him.

Everyone grew frantic. The person who said they'd
"seen this before" revealed they meant they'd seen it
at a service at another church. Others who were new
to the talks misunderstood, and assumed the person
meant Matsuo had collapsed before. When some
people tried to help Matsu, others shouted, "Don't get
in the way!" and, "If you interrupt he may die." Some
attendees thought the collapse was part of a staged
act, that this was proof that we were some shady cult,
and they were shouting out of anger and disillusion-
ment. There was total chaos.

"IT WAS SOMETHING of a blind spot we had,"
Mineno said quietly. She seemed scared. "Since
we didn't get too involved with the participants and
simply gathered instead, no one really knew anyone
else . . . If we'd had officers to manage the group, it
probably would have been easier to handle the situation. And at the time, Matsuo-san's wife, Yo-chan-san,
was out . . ."

THOSE WHO TRIED to rush to Matsuo were stopped by force. Folding chairs collapsed and confusion spread. Thanks to Yoshida, who called an ambulance, medics soon arrived, but some of the audience members tried to stop them from coming in. Fights broke out. The paramedics must have been confused. There was screaming and weeping. But gradually attitudes changed as people realized the old man really had collapsed. Eventually, they managed to get Matsuo on a stretcher.

Matsuo's life was saved, but he could no longer move his left arm. If he had made it to the hospital a little sooner, they might have been able to prevent that. But Matsuo didn't blame anyone. No one had done anything wrong. Those who'd mistaken what was happening for a spiritual phenomenon—those people who had experienced so much unhappiness and hoped to be saved—they only wished it could be the truth. They saw things the way they did because of their pure desire to be saved by something great. One could even say that Matsuo's paralyzed left arm was born out of their suffering. "This isn't enough," Matsuo later said. "One left arm can't take on all their suffering. Not that I have the right to do that, anyway."

Since that incident five years ago, the talks had changed. Many people were disappointed that Matsuo was not holy, and others put distance between themselves and the group after experiencing that strange disturbance.

While Matsuo was in the hospital, people still assembled every second Saturday, hung around for a while even though there were no lectures. That's when Sawatari showed up. He'd watched the uproar when Matsuo collapsed, unmoved. He saw that those frantic people who believed Matsuo had actually been possessed would be easy to manipulate. Yoshida watched from afar as Sawatari made his way among the gathered crowd, talking to people. In less than a half hour, he had collected a group of people who were crying in front of him. That day, Sawatari took about fifty participants with him and vanished. Many of the people who followed him were highly educated. Later they would realize they still had more to learn about him.

"MATSUO-SAN WAS SCAMMED," Mineno said quietly. "Someone asked him to donate part of the land he owned for a charity hospital, and without thinking much about it, he handed it over. But that land was never used for a hospital. Before he knew it, it was sold and resold, and was eventually used to build a highway. But that's not all. We don't know the details, but the contract he'd signed had a stipulation sneaked in that required him to give up more and more, and he suffered a pretty big loss. The scam was carried out by a sham investment firm Sawatari was involved with. Matsuo-san doesn't like to talk about it—really, none of us know anything about Matsuo-san's life before he showed up at the mansion—but it seems Matsuo-san and Sawatari have a long history together. Anyway, Sawatari took a chunk of Matsuo-san's property and a bunch of the people who used to come here and vanished. And . . ." Mineno suddenly went quiet.

Yoshida finished the story. "That woman you're looking for, she was involved with that investment firm. She's one of the people who scammed Matsuo-san. She vanished with Sawatari—or maybe it's more accurate to say they returned to their own cult."

"Their own cult?" Narazaki repeated.

"Yes. She's not here. They're part of a nameless cult. They came to the attention of the Public Security Bureau once, and after that they went underground. It seems the Bureau just calls them X, since they have no name. It's a pretty frightening name. Maybe there's some other reason they use it, but I'm not sure. The woman you're searching for, and we're searching for, is there."

# Other Titles in the Soho Crime Series

**STEPHANIE BARRON**
(Jane Austen's England)
Jane and the Twelve Days
   of Christmas
Jane and the Waterloo Map
Jane and the Year Without a Summer

**F.H. BATACAN**
(Philippines)
Smaller and Smaller Circles

**JAMES R. BENN**
(World War II Europe)
Billy Boyle
The First Wave
Blood Alone
Evil for Evil
Rag & Bone
A Mortal Terror
Death's Door
A Blind Goddess
The Rest Is Silence
The White Ghost
Blue Madonna
The Devouring
Solemn Graves
When Hell Struck Twelve
The Red Horse
Road of Bones
From the Shadows

The Refusal Camp: Stories

**CARA BLACK**
(Paris, France)
Murder in the Marais
Murder in Belleville
Murder in the Sentier
Murder in the Bastille
Murder in Clichy
Murder in Montmartre
Murder on the Ile Saint-Louis
Murder in the Rue de Paradis
Murder in the Latin Quarter
Murder in the Palais Royal
Murder in Passy
Murder at the Lanterne Rouge
Murder Below Montparnasse
Murder in Pigalle
Murder on the Champ de Mars
Murder on the Quai
Murder in Saint-Germain
Murder on the Left Bank

**CARA BLACK CONT.**
Murder in Bel-Air
Murder at the Porte de Versailles

Three Hours in Paris
Night Flight to Paris

**HENRY CHANG**
(Chinatown)
Chinatown Beat
Year of the Dog
Red Jade
Death Money
Lucky

**BARBARA CLEVERLY**
(England)
The Last Kashmiri Rose
Strange Images of Death
The Blood Royal
Not My Blood
A Spider in the Cup
Enter Pale Death
Diana's Altar

Fall of Angels
Invitation to Die

**COLIN COTTERILL**
(Laos)
The Coroner's Lunch
Thirty-Three Teeth
Disco for the Departed
Anarchy and Old Dogs
Curse of the Pogo Stick
The Merry Misogynist
Love Songs from a Shallow Grave
Slash and Burn
The Woman Who Wouldn't Die
Six and a Half Deadly Sins
I Shot the Buddha
The Rat Catchers' Olympics
Don't Eat Me
The Second Biggest Nothing
The Delightful Life of
   a Suicide Pilot

The Motion Picture Teller

**ELI CRANOR**
(Arkansas)
Don't Know Tough
Ozark Dogs

**GARRY DISHER**
(Australia)
The Dragon Man
Kittyhawk Down
Snapshot
Chain of Evidence
Blood Moon
Whispering Death
Signal Loss

Wyatt
Port Vila Blues
Fallout

Under the Cold Bright Lights

**TERESA DOVALPAGE**
(Cuba)
Death Comes in through
   the Kitchen
Queen of Bones
Death under the Perseids

Death of a Telenovela Star
   (A Novella)

**DAVID DOWNING**
(World War II Germany)
Zoo Station
Silesian Station
Stettin Station
Potsdam Station
Lehrter Station
Masaryk Station
Wedding Station

(World War I)
Jack of Spies
One Man's Flag
Lenin's Roller Coaster
The Dark Clouds Shining

Diary of a Dead Man on Leave

**RAMONA EMERSON**
(Navajo Nation)
Shutter

**AGNETE FRIIS**
(Denmark)
What My Body Remembers
The Summer of Ellen

## TIMOTHY HALLINAN
(Thailand)
The Fear Artist
For the Dead
The Hot Countries
Fools' River
Street Music

(Los Angeles)
Crashed
Little Elvises
The Fame Thief
Herbie's Game
King Maybe
Fields Where They Lay
Nighttown
Rock of Ages

## METTE IVIE HARRISON
(Mormon Utah)
The Bishop's Wife
His Right Hand
For Time and All Eternities
Not of This Fold
The Prodigal Daughter

## MICK HERRON
(England)
Slow Horses
Dead Lions
The List (A Novella)
Real Tigers
Spook Street
London Rules
The Marylebone Drop (A Novella)
Joe Country
The Catch (A Novella)
Slough House
Bad Actors

Down Cemetery Road
The Last Voice You Hear
Why We Die
Smoke and Whispers

Reconstruction
Nobody Walks
This Is What Happened
Dolphin Junction: Stories

## NAOMI HIRAHARA
(Japantown)
Clark and Division

## STAN JONES
(Alaska)
White Sky, Black Ice
Shaman Pass
Frozen Sun
Village of the Ghost Bears
Tundra Kill
The Big Empty

## STEVEN MACK JONES
(Detroit)
August Snow
Lives Laid Away
Dead of Winter

## LENE KAABERBØL & AGNETE FRIIS
(Denmark)
The Boy in the Suitcase
Invisible Murder
Death of a Nightingale
The Considerate Killer

## MARTIN LIMÓN
(South Korea)
Jade Lady Burning
Slicky Boys
Buddha's Money
The Door to Bitterness
The Wandering Ghost
G.I. Bones
Mr. Kill
The Joy Brigade
Nightmare Range
The Iron Sickle
The Ville Rat
Ping-Pong Heart
The Nine-Tailed Fox
The Line
GI Confidential
War Women

## ED LIN
(Taiwan)
Ghost Month
Incensed
99 Ways to Die
Death Doesn't Forget

## PETER LOVESEY
(England)
The Circle
The Headhunters
False Inspector Dew
Rough Cider
On the Edge
The Reaper

## PETER LOVESEY CONT.
(Bath, England)
The Last Detective
Diamond Solitaire
The Summons
Bloodhounds
Upon a Dark Night
The Vault
Diamond Dust
The House Sitter
The Secret Hangman
Skeleton Hill
Stagestruck
Cop to Corpse
The Tooth Tattoo
The Stone Wife
Down Among the Dead Men
Another One Goes Tonight
Beau Death
Killing with Confetti
The Finisher
Diamond and the Eye
Showstopper

(London, England)
Wobble to Death
The Detective Wore
Silk Drawers
Abracadaver
Mad Hatter's Holiday
The Tick of Death
A Case of Spirits
Swing, Swing Together
Waxwork

Bertie and the Tinman
Bertie and the Seven Bodies
Bertie and the Crime of Passion

## SUJATA MASSEY
(1920s Bombay)
The Widows of Malabar Hill
The Satapur Moonstone
The Bombay Prince

## FRANCINE MATHEWS
(Nantucket)
Death in the Off-Season
Death in Rough Water
Death in a Mood Indigo
Death in a Cold Hard Light
Death on Nantucket
Death on Tuckernuck
Death on a Winter Stroll

**SEICHŌ MATSUMOTO**
(Japan)
*Inspector Imanishi Investigates*

**CHRIS MCKINNEY**
(Post Apocalyptic Future)
*Midnight, Water City*

**MAGDALEN NABB**
(Italy)
*Death of an Englishman*
*Death of a Dutchman*
*Death in Springtime*
*Death in Autumn*
*The Marshal and the Murderer*
*The Marshal and the Madwoman*
*The Marshal's Own Case*
*The Marshal Makes His Report*
*The Marshal at the Villa Torrini*
*Property of Blood*
*Some Bitter Taste*
*The Innocent*
*Vita Nuova*
*The Monster of Florence*

**FUMINORI NAKAMURA**
(Japan)
*The Thief*
*Evil and the Mask*
*Last Winter, We Parted*
*The Kingdom*
*The Boy in the Earth*
*Cult X*
*My Annihilation*
*The Rope Artist*

**STUART NEVILLE**
(Northern Ireland)
*The Ghosts of Belfast*
*Collusion*
*Stolen Souls*
*The Final Silence*
*Those We Left Behind*
*So Say the Fallen*

*The Traveller & Other Stories*
*House of Ashes*

(Dublin)
*Ratlines*

**KWEI QUARTEY**
(Ghana)
*Murder at Cape Three Points*
*Gold of Our Fathers*
*Death by His Grace*

**KWEI QUARTEY CONT.**
*The Missing American*
*Sleep Well, My Lady*
*Last Seen in Lapaz*

**QIU XIAOLONG**
(China)
*Death of a Red Heroine*
*A Loyal Character Dancer*
*When Red Is Black*

**MARCIE R. RENDON**
(Minnesota's Red River Valley)
*Murder on the Red River*
*Girl Gone Missing*
*Sinister Graves*

**JAMES SALLIS**
(New Orleans)
*The Long-Legged Fly*
*Moth*
*Black Hornet*
*Eye of the Cricket*
*Bluebottle*
*Ghost of a Flea*

*Sarah Jane*

**JOHN STRALEY**
(Sitka, Alaska)
*The Woman Who Married a Bear*
*The Curious Eat Themselves*
*The Music of What Happens*
*Death and the Language*
  *of Happiness*
*The Angels Will Not Care*
*Cold Water Burning*
*Baby's First Felony*
*So Far and Good*

(Cold Storage, Alaska)
*The Big Both Ways*
*Cold Storage, Alaska*
*What Is Time to a Pig?*
*Blown by the Same Wind*

**AKIMITSU TAKAGI**
(Japan)
*The Tattoo Murder Case*
*Honeymoon to Nowhere*
*The Informer*

**CAMILLA TRINCHIERI**
(Tuscany)
*Murder in Chianti*
*The Bitter Taste of Murder*
*Murder on the Vine*

**HELENE TURSTEN**
(Sweden)
*Detective Inspector Huss*
*The Torso*
*The Glass Devil*
*Night Rounds*
*The Golden Calf*
*The Fire Dance*
*The Beige Man*
*The Treacherous Net*
*Who Watcheth*
*Protected by the Shadows*

*Hunting Game*
*Winter Grave*
*Snowdrift*

*An Elderly Lady Is Up*
  *to No Good*
*An Elderly Lady Must Not*
  *Be Crossed*

**ILARIA TUTI**
(Italy)
*Flowers over the Inferno*
*The Sleeping Nymph*

**JANWILLEM VAN DE WETERING**
(Holland)
*Outsider in Amsterdam*
*Tumbleweed*
*The Corpse on the Dike*
*Death of a Hawker*
*The Japanese Corpse*
*The Blond Baboon*
*The Maine Massacre*
*The Mind-Murders*
*The Streetbird*
*The Rattle-Rat*
*Hard Rain*
*Just a Corpse at Twilight*
*Hollow-Eyed Angel*
*The Perfidious Parrot*
*The Sergeant's Cat:*
  *Collected Stories*

**JACQUELINE WINSPEAR**
(1920s England)
*Maisie Dobbs*
*Birds of a Feather*